"It is time to perform the rites of sacrifice," Malory said. "Please join hands. Tonight we will visit Eve Camlan to begin preparing her as a gift."

"Does it really have to be Eve?" Heather asked.

"It must. She has the right vibrations, she has power of a sort, and she's a virgin," Malory said. "Don't worry. The fact that she is so dear to you will make her an even better sacrifice. We shall receive many years of grace in exchange for her life."

Heather nodded.

Malory looked at each girl in turn. "Now, everyone concentrate on sending your power to me so that I can show her the first dream."

Everyone but Malory and Brittany closed their eyes. Malory began to chant, never breaking the power-inducing gaze she shared with Brittany. After a few minutes, the static electricity in the room grew so strong that Brittany could feel her hair trying to lift away from her arms and scalp.

Suddenly, there was an audible snap of electricity and all their robes fell from their shoulders. The room swirled with energy; Brittany basked in it. She could see the hair rising on the other girls and slowly, she felt gravity lose its grip.

"Eve," Malory whispered. "What scares you, Eve?"

She closed her eyes and Brittany saw that she knew. . . .

Books by Tamara Thorne

HAUNTED

MOONFALL

ETERNITY

CANDLE BAY

BAD THINGS

THE FORGOTTEN

The Sorority Trilogy
EVE

Published by Pinnacle Books

⊰THE SORORITY⊱
EVE

TAMARA THORNE

PINNACLE BOOKS
Kensington Publishing Corp.
http://www.kensingtonbooks.com

PINNACLE BOOKS are published by

Kensington Publishing Corp.
850 Third Avenue
New York, NY 10022

All Kensington Titles, Imprints, and Distributed Lines are available at special quantity discounts for bulk purchases for sales promotions, premiums, fund-raising, and educational or institutional use. Special book excerpts or customized printings can also be created to fit specific needs. For details, write or phone the office of the Kensington special sales manager: Kensington Publishing Corp., 850 Third Avenue, New York, NY 10022, attn: Special Sales Department. Phone: 1-800-221-2647.

Pinnacle and the P logo Reg. U.S. Pat. & TM Off.

First Pinnacle Books Printing: June 2003

10 9 8 7 6 5 4 3 2 1

Printed in the United States of America

To the memory of my mother
Who told me stories of a real town
drowned beneath a lake;
Of what it was like to live there before,
and to swim above it, after.

ACKNOWLEDGMENTS

I'll save most of my thanks for Part Three of this trilogy, but special nods go to Q.L. Pearce, who knows which books to lend me before I even know to ask, and to Bill Gagliani, whom I've yet to stump with weird questions. Thank you as well to John, Damien, and Kay. Finally, a tip of the hat goes to the makers of all those cheerleader and sorority horror movies and to Sir Thomas Malory and his ilk for some peculiar bits of inspiration.

Applehead Lake Cheerleading Camp

EIGHT YEARS AGO

1

"They say she's still down there." Merilynn Morris trailed her fingers through the cool summer water as Samantha and Eve dipped their oars, slowly paddling toward the little island in the center of the lake. "She's still down there, trapped. Waiting."

"Waiting for what?" asked Sam. "Prince Charming?"

Merilynn looked up at Samantha Penrose and Eve Camlan with eyes so green that when they first met, Eve thought she wore colored contact lenses. But she didn't, and contacts couldn't do what Merilynn's eyes could do. Now they appeared to change from the deep shades of the shadowy forest to that of brilliant emeralds. At the sight, even scared-of-nothing Sam stopped giggling.

Merilynn looked far older than her eight years as she regarded them. "Prince Charming's for little kids—" she said archly.

"I kno-ow," Sam interrupted. "I was joking.

Who cares about dumb old Prince Charming, anyway?"

Eve did, but she didn't say so. She'd already figured out that Sam, who was pretty much a tomboy, and almost a whole year older, would think she was a wimp if she talked about handsome princes and beautiful princesses, about dragons and knights and true love. And Merilynn? She wouldn't tease, probably, but she'd do that weird, serene smile of hers, like in those paintings by the Old Misters.

In fact, Eve had no idea what went on in the green-eyed girl's mind, but it was something mysterious, interesting, and a little spooky. Like the way she could change the color of her eyes. Eve thought it was magic, but when she said so, Merilynn had a giggle fit. For an instant, Eve thought she was going to make fun of her, but instead she said thank you and kissed her forehead, which was another weird but kind of nice thing Merilynn did sometimes.

"Holly Gayle," Merilynn said, sitting up straight in the little boat but looking down into the dark water, "is waiting to smite the evildoers who drowned her town and murdered her for her treasure."

"Smite?" asked Eve. "What's 'smite'?"

"It's something God does," Sam said. "It's like squishing a bug."

"Eww."

Samantha grinned, somberness all gone.

"Yeah, Evie, this giant hand comes down out of the clouds thumb first, and starts squashing people." She demonstrated on her knee. "But that's not real and neither is any old treasure. I've been hearing this story since the first night of camp, and there's no treasure. That's just a fairy tale. Probably, Holly Gayle wasn't ever real either."

"It's all true," Merilynn said solemnly. "Holly Gayle was real. She's at the bottom of the lake. She's waiting." Late afternoon sun reflected on the lake water and blazed through her red hair.

"Merilynn, you're giving me the creeps," Eve said, glancing at the sky, involuntarily shivering as a cloud edged in front of the sun. "Maybe we should get back. It might rain and we need to practice our cheers."

Sam rolled her eyes to the sky. "It's not going to rain and we're almost there. Paddle faster. I want to see the island—we might not get another chance."

Eve nodded and did as Samantha ordered. She couldn't let spooky stories stop her now. The three had planned this trip to Applehead Island for two days, and now, while just about everybody was on a field trip to Greenbriar University, on the other side of the lake, was the only time they could get away with it.

"Why do you think the island is off-limits?" Eve asked as they drew near the rocky tree-topped oasis. They were close enough that she

could make out misshapen apples on a few of
the ancient, arthritic trees. Years ago, there
were orchards here. Now the rest of the trees
were under the lake. Could they still grow apples? *Dark orchard, tree limbs reaching in vain
toward the sun as they drown.* She shivered. "The
counselors sounded really serious when they
said we couldn't come out here."

"It's haunted," Merilynn said, staring past Eve
at the island.

"Shut up!" Samantha said, laughing. "You'll
scare her. Eve, it's off-limits because it's a make-
out spot. Our counselors meet the counselors
from the football camp out here at night." She
giggled. "We'll probably find all sorts of nasty
things up there."

"Nasty?" Eve asked, delighted, her fears forgotten.

"Yep. Like blankets and underwear and stuff."

"And condoms," Merilynn added sagely.

"Huh?" Eve asked as Sam cracked up.

"You don't know what condoms are?" She
pushed long titian hair from her face.

"I know," Sam said. "My parents have them
in the bottom drawer of my mom's nightstand."
She giggled some more. "They have all kinds
of weird stuff in that drawer. I think it's sex
stuff."

"But what are condoms?" Eve asked, pleased
that know-it-all Sam didn't really know after all.
"Come on, Merilynn."

Laughter tinkled down the scale and the girl's green eyes glowed with mischief. "They're for *sex,*" she said.

"And?" Sam urged.

"Guys stick 'em on their thingies so they don't get girls pregnant when they stick it in."

"When they *what?*" Eve gasped.

"Stick it in." Merilynn was controlling her giggles, but just barely. "Eve, don't you know what sexual intercourse is?"

Eve shook her head.

Samantha cleared her throat. "You know those boring cartoons they show us about how guys' sperms go in and look for your egg so they can make a baby?"

Eve remembered the stupid drawings, all right. What a snore. "So?"

"What do you think those cartoons are supposed to be?"

"Bodies," Eve said slowly. She shook blond hair out of her face.

"*Whose* bodies?" Merilynn asked.

"'Toons' bodies, how should I know?" Eve glanced at Sam, who was red-faced, shaking, and just about ready to explode. "What's so funny? Whose bodies, Sam?"

"Grown-ups." Sam snorted and started giggling again.

"You guys don't know anything, do you?" Merilynn said. "After you get your period and your boobies grow, you want boys to stick it in you.

They have to wear condoms so that you don't make babies."

"Ewwwww!" Sam and Eve cried in unison.

"Your parents *do it*, Sam," Merilynn said happily. "They have condoms. That's proof. Both your parents did it and didn't use condoms, because if they did you wouldn't have gotten made."

"So our counselors are doing it on the island?" Sam asked. "With *boys?*"

"Well, if they're not doing with boys, we won't find any condoms. And you know what that means?" Merilynn twinkled.

"What?" Sam asked.

"They're lezzies."

"Oh, gross!" Eve wasn't positive what lezzies were, but was pretty sure it was disgusting.

"We should spy on them," Sam said.

"We can't," Eve said. Sam wanted to spy on everybody. She always wanted to know everything about everyone, which was kind of fun, but no way did Eve want to be on Applehead Island after dark. "They'd know the boat was gone when they go to come out here."

"No," Sam said. "I mean, let's look in the counselors' cabin after they go to bed and see what they're doing."

"Okay," Merilynn said, carefully standing. "We're here." She jumped out of the boat into thigh-deep water. "Woo! Cold!" She walked to the pointy end and yanked it forward, onto the narrow beach. "Help me!"

The others got out and together they pulled
the rowboat up far enough to be sure it wouldn't
float away.

"We need to hurry," Eve said.

"Why?" Sam asked. "It's only about four o'clock.
They won't be back from the field trip until five-
thirty, at least."

"Look at the sky," Merilynn said.

Overhead, clouds dotted the sky now, puffy
white on top but gray and flat on the bottom.
"Where'd those come from?" Eve asked. "A few
minutes ago, there was only one."

Merilynn giggled. "Maybe it had babies."

"Come on, you guys." Sam had already hiked
up the little hill and was looking back down at
them. "Follow me." She turned and started
walking.

Merilynn glanced at Eve and stepped forward,
but Eve put her hand out and touched her arm.
"Can I ask you a question?"

"Sure." Merilynn looked into her eyes. "Anything."

"How come you're here? I mean, you said your
father is, well, a Father."

"A priest," Merilynn said. "That's right."

"So, he doesn't have sex."

"Well, he's really my uncle Martin. He adopted
me when I was a baby after his brother—my dad
and my mom—got killed in a car accident."

"But you call him 'Father,'" Eve said.

Merilynn's nose crinkled in a pixyish grin.

"Everybody calls him 'Father' because he's a priest. I do too because I think of him as my real father, but I could call him Uncle Martin if I wanted."

"But he's a priest. Isn't that wrong or something, calling him Father?"

Merilynn shrugged. "I don't think so. He doesn't mind. He says he gets the best of both worlds because he's a Father *and* a father."

"Are you guys coming or what?" Sam's voice called from somewhere above.

"In a second," Merilynn yelled. "Listen, Eve, I'll tell you a secret, but you have to promise not to tell."

"Even Sam?"

"Yes, even Sam, because she'd start playing Lois Lane or something and snooping too much, and this is private. It's probably not even true, but I think it is. I have a hunch it is."

"What?" Eve's hand tightened on her friend's arm. "Cross my heart, I won't tell."

"Okay. I think Father isn't my uncle. I think he's my real father. As in, once he had sex and didn't use a condom."

"But he's a priest," Eve protested, shocked. "You mean he had you before he was a priest?"

"No. He's been a priest for like twelve or thirteen years."

"Then he couldn't be your father. He can't have sex."

Merilynn bent forward and kissed Eve's forehead again. "No, Evie. He *could* have sex, he's just not supposed to. I think some beautiful fairy queen made love to him when he was asleep."

"You mean like an angel?"

Merilynn nodded somberly. "Yes, only I think angels don't have anything, you know, *down there,* so it was a fairy queen. They've got lady parts and so she got pregnant and had me, but couldn't take care of me in the fairy kingdom, so she left me with him. And he made up the story about my real mother and father dying when I was only a few days old to cover it all up. Because they probably wouldn't let him be a priest anymore if they knew the truth."

"But—"

"But nothing, Evie. I looked everywhere. On the Net and in Father's pictures from when he was little. He had a brother just a couple years younger than him that's in the photos up until Father was about ten, but then there's no sign of him. No more pictures. I think maybe he died a really long time ago."

"Do you have a grandma you can ask?"

"No. Nobody but Father." She started walking, Eve beside her. "It's just a theory of mine."

"It's nice," Eve said. "I see why you don't want Sam to know, besides the snooping part."

Merilynn paused. "Why?"

"She'd think the fairy goddess mother was silly."

Merilynn nodded and took Eve's hand as they

reached the top of the hill. "She would think it was silly. But she'd be wrong."

"Yes," Eve said, squeezing Merilynn's hand. "She'd be wrong."

2

Applehead Island was so named because it was a lump of land shaped kind of like an ugly head poking out of the water. It rose maybe a total of twenty feet out of the lake at its peak, and scraggly old half-dead apple trees stuck out of the upper reaches like spiky hair. From the lake's edge, at times of day when the sun hit it just right, it really looked like a face, from the nose up. A jetty of land at water's edge stuck out like a nose on the side facing the cheerleading camp, and above it, two rocky hollows peered, eyelike, toward shore. Then, a little above, the trees poked up like bristly hair. From shore, Eve, Sam, Merilynn, and some of the other campers loved telling ghost stories about the face, like how it was the head of a giant and he'd walk to shore at three in the morning and peep into the cabins (that part, the peeping part, was Sam's idea of course). If you were foolish enough to be outside when he came ashore, he'd snatch you and take you back to his underwater town and keep you there with Holly Gayle and the treasure forever.

Or maybe eat you, if you preferred Sam's version of the story.

But from here, standing between gnarled old trees with their litter of puny greenish apples, the island wasn't all that spooky. But the water was. The sky, filling with gray-bottomed clouds, made the lake look black and fathomless. Here and there sunlight still hit the water in little lightninglike flashes, but that didn't make it any cheerier. Pretty much the opposite, Eve thought, shivering. "There's a whole town down there," she said.

"Yes," Merilynn said softly. "It's still there. It's been there forever."

"And lots of trees." Sam jumped down from a boulder behind them. "It's only been there since 1906," she said. "I looked it up. They flooded the valley to make this reservoir that year."

"And killed all the people," Eve sighed, feeling a delicious little tremor run through her.

"No, they didn't. That's just made-up stuff," Sam said. "Everyone had already moved out. Most of the people went to settle in Caledonia, and some moved to the other side, near the university, and created a new town and named it Greenbriar, after the university."

"Some town," Eve said. "A gas station, a dinky store with a post office inside it, and a motel. Bor-ring."

"There're some houses and stuff," Merilynn said. "But you're right, Evie. It's pretty dinky."

"There used to be more stuff there," Sam told them. "More people and more businesses. There was even a church."

"The church is still there," Merilynn said, pointing toward the far side of the lake. "In the woods behind the university. It's a ruin now, haunted by the green ghost. The Forest Knight. There are still some old deserted cottages in the woods, too. They say the people just disappeared from them. Left their food on the table and fires in the hearths and just—pop!—vanished into thin air. Maybe the green ghost took them. Or the people who trapped Holly Gayle. They're still here, too. Their ghosts, or maybe even the actual people. Maybe they were Druids and they never die. No one knows for sure."

Sam rolled her eyes. "That's nonsense, Merilynn, old silly stories. But there really was a church. And a school, too."

"Greenbriar University is a school," Eve said, glad that Sam thought Merilynn's stories were made up.

"I mean a regular kids' school, not a college. A public school."

"Where'd all the people go?" Merilynn prodded, with a slight smile. "I mean if they didn't mysteriously disappear in the forest."

"Nobody 'mysteriously disappeared' unless maybe bears ate them or they murdered each other," Sam said. "They left because it's nicer on the coast. It's easier to get to, on a main road, and there are more places to work. And Caledonia's pretty; probably most of them went there, or down to Red Cay to start fishing businesses. Some must have gone to live in San Francisco."

"It's nice *here,*" Merilynn countered, gesturing around. "A lake, forests all around, ancient oak trees, pine trees, squirrels—"

"Nuts." Sam laughed.

Sam was pretty for a tomboy, with sable-brown eyes and thick dark hair that would look really good if she'd let Eve style it for her.

"Samantha," Eve said firmly, "Merilynn's right. It's nice here. Maybe the people moved away because of a curse."

"The curse of Holly Gayle," Merilynn added.

"You two." Sam shook her head. "Okay. There was *maybe* a coed at the university named Holly Gayle, and *maybe* she drowned—"

"Was murdered," said Merilynn.

"*Maybe.* Whatever, the records that far back were mostly destroyed in a fire in the administration building. There's no proof."

"She's down there," Merilynn said calmly. "Sometimes, late at night, you can hear her calling for help from the old drowned ghost town under the lake, where they imprisoned her forever."

"Or until somebody can set her free," Eve added, trying to make the ideal more appealing to no-nonsense Sam. It didn't help.

"Who captured her?" Sam asked, grinning. "Satanists?"

Merilynn made a face. "Of course not. Satanists are, like, *sooo* boring. The people that captured her were Druids or something. They worshipped the old gods."

"Older-than-God gods?" Eve asked.

Merilynn nodded, eyes sparkling. "The day Holly Gayle is released from bondage, all these old trees will grow leaves like crazy and make a ton of big sweet fruit. The green ghost in the chapel in the woods will make all the flowers bloom again and kill all the old icky Druids who are still around here, hiding. Only I don't think they're Druids exactly. Father says old-time Druids sacrificed people and animals all the time for the old gods, so I guess they were bad, but Christians were always slaughtering lambs and stuff, and that one guy killed his kid for God—"

"And God let people kill Jesus, his very own kid," Sam added. "I think that's just as bad. I think it's just the same, in fact. No offense, Merilynn, but religion is creepy."

Merilynn nodded slowly. "Yeah, I know. Well, whatever they were, the ones who caught Holly Gayle, they worshipped old gods and the green ghost is going to kill them."

Sam snorted. "Why? I thought old gods liked Druids. Why would he kill them? Isn't he supposed to be an old god?"

"Is he?" asked Eve. "An old god?"

"I don't know. Maybe. He was a magical knight, I think. I never thought about it." Merilynn looked thoughtful. "Besides, maybe they aren't Druids. Or maybe they're *evil* Druids."

"You're Catholic," Sam said. "What do you know about Druids and stuff? Isn't that a sin or something, to know that stuff?"

Merilynn looked solemn. "Father studies lots of things like that and he tells me about them. He says knowledge isn't a sin unless you use it to do bad things."

"He's one weird priest," said Sam.

"Yeah," Merilynn agreed. "Isn't that great?"

Eve was watching the sky darken with clouds. "We should go soon. I want to practice my cheers."

"Come on, let's just see what's around over there." Sam pointed at some rocky outcroppings that hid more of the little island. "Real quick, I promise."

"There's supposed to be a cave," Merilynn said.

"Cool." Sam started hiking and the other two followed.

"Look!" Eve pointed at a dark grotto twenty feet beyond the rocky projection.

"The cave," Merilynn said, scrambling forward.

Eve followed the other two, hoping it wasn't really a cave. Sort of hoping, anyway. Black lake water gleamed darkly and she thought about the town below. How many houses had there been? Were there farms and orchards and stores and a schoolhouse, like on *Little House* reruns? Were there ghosts?

"Merilynn, don't go too close," Sam said.

Eve turned to look at the cave thingy. It looked like a ring of rocks sticking up from the ground against the hill, which hung over it like a little cliff, twisted apple tree roots hanging down like skeletal fingers. Merilynn was leaning over the rocks, looking down. "I don't think it's very deep," she said. "But I can't see because it's really dark in there. Stupid clouds. I wish we'd brought a flashlight." She wiggled up higher, her feet leaving the ground as she tilted herself down to get a better look.

"Well, we didn't bring one," Sam said as she and Eve both looked into the fissure. "Don't go falling in there, Merilynn. You'll land in old panties and condoms and stuff."

That worked; Merilynn stood up and stepped back. "Yuck. But maybe it's a cave. Maybe Holly Gayle's down there somewhere. We'll have to come back."

Wind gusted, blowing their hair into their eyes, making sparse leaves on old apple trees sputter. And a long, low wail rose from within the dark grotto. It seemed to spiral up and out, until it built into a banshee scream. Eve and Merilynn scuttled backward, and even Sam jumped away from the hole. "It's just the wind," she said, but she didn't sound too convinced. "Let's get back before it rains." She pushed her fingers against Eve's shoulder. "Get going!"

Without another word, Eve took off, scrambling

back around the rocks, spurred on by the wailing sound that grew even louder behind them. She moved quickly, earth trickling down the hillside under her sneakers. Suddenly, her foot caught under an exposed tree root and she went down, landing hard on her knees and hands. "Ow!"

Sam nearly fell over her but managed to leap to the right, barely touching her. Instantly, she turned and crouched. "Are you okay?"

Eve looked up at her and nodded; then Sam stood and offered her hand. Eve slapped her own together, brushing off twigs and dirt, then took Sam's to help her stand up. "Ouch," she said, becoming aware of stinging pain in one knee. She put her foot on a rock and checked out the damage.

"Now *that's* what I call a skinned knee," Sam said admiringly.

"Oh, eww. It's ugly and it hurts." Her stomach twisted—the knee was nasty and bloody, pocked with dirt and debris. Cringing, but determined not to get all shaky in front of Sam, Eve started to pick pebbles and leaf out of the wound, but then she saw something moving. "Oh, God," she whispered. "Oh, God, oh God, oh God. Sam, get it off me!"

"What?"

"That!" She pointed at the thing. "Hurry! I think I'm going to faint!"

Sam bent, then reached out and plucked the

thing off, held it out. "It's just an earthworm," she said. "You're not going to faint."

"Get it away from me. I don't want to see it!"

"Jeez, Evie, it's not even a whole worm, just part of one. See?"

"Oh, gross! *Please* get rid of it! Now!"

Sam put the worm down in some leaves by the tree root while Eve picked more gunk off her knee, gravel and bits of leaves. "I hope it doesn't scar," she said.

"It's not going to scar. It's just your stupid knee!" Sam looked around. "Where's Merilynn?"

"I don't know!" Another banshee howl suddenly tore the air. Eve forgot about the injury and hugged herself tightly. "Merilynn!" she yelled, but her voice was stolen by the wind.

"Stay put," Sam told her and started back toward the rocks. "I'll get her." Eve nodded, happy to stay behind.

Long minutes passed, and the howling rose and fell as the tree branches whipped up and the sky turned a uniform steel gray. The lake shimmered, a black mirror cracked with low-ridged whitecaps. Across the water, a mist was rising in the dark, haunted woods. She could barely see the camp's short dock, and the tall flagpole was invisible except for the American flag at the top. The green and gold camp flag blended in with the trees. They had to row all the way back across the black lake, and the thought terrified her as much as the howls of wind that echoed all around now, calling across the water like hungry wolves. *Stop it! You can't be scared! Sam'll make fun of you. She might tell the others and then they'll all make fun of you!*

"Samantha?" she called, suddenly. "Merilynn? Hurry up!" Shivering from both cold and fear, she took tentative steps back toward the cave. A heavy raindrop splatted on her forearm, followed a few seconds later by another. "You guys? Are you okay?"

She thought she heard Sam's voice, but wasn't positive. "You guys? Sam? It's starting to rain!" She climbed around the outcropping and saw Samantha, well, saw everything but her head and shoulders because she was bending over, looking down into the rock-lined hole or cave or whatever it was.

"Sam?" she called from a dozen feet away.

"Eve! Get over here!"

Eve barely heard her since Sam didn't look up, but she rushed to join her, instantly positive Merilynn had fallen into the hole and Sam was trying to rescue her. But as she arrived, she saw the other girl had only been hidden in the shadows of dangling roots on the far side of the opening. She, too, was looking down into the darkness, bent so far over that none of her coppery hair was visible.

A dozen raindrops spattered on Eve's face. "What are you doing, you guys? We have to get back. Hurry up! It's raining!"

Sam raised her head and looked at Eve. "Look!" She turned back. "Look!"

The howling wind still came from all around, from the forest across the lake, from the trees on the island; if it had been the banshee shriek from the grotto, Eve couldn't have made herself look into that dark hole again. Swallowing hard, she gripped the rocky edge. Across from her, Merilynn glanced up and smiled, eyes dancing with emerald light.

The sun is gone. How can her eyes do that?

It had only lasted an instant; already, Merilynn had dipped her head back down. Deciding she'd imagined the light, Eve closed her eyes and held her breath, as if she were diving into the lake, then tilted her neck down, her face to the darkness.

And opened her eyes.

The perfect darkness was broken only by two tiny sparkling dabs of green deep, deep down. Eve stared. "What are those lights?" she murmured, too fascinated to be afraid.

"I don't know," Sam said softly. "Lights. Maybe glowing rocks?"

"No." Merilynn spoke in a near whisper.

The emerald chips winked out for a split second, then came back on.

"It's an animal," Sam said. "Like a mountain lion or a bobcat. Cats' eyes glow in the dark."

"It's trapped down there?" Concern washed over Eve. "We have to tell someone and get it rescued. Poor kitty."

"It's not trapped," Sam said. I'm sure there's an entrance lower down, probably on the other side of the island."

"Then it's dangerous to be here if it's a mountain lion," Eve said.

"Shh!" Merilynn looked up, the green sparks in her eyes the same shade as the green dabs far below. "It's not a mountain lion. It's not an animal."

"What is it, then?" Sam asked.

"Look," Merilynn replied. "Look at them."

And Eve realized that the twin green lights were slowly but surely growing larger.

Coming closer. "Sam, we should leave *right* now." She clutched her wrist, but both of them continued to watch the lights' slow movement.

"What is it, Merilynn?" Sam asked.

"I'm not sure. The green ghost? Holly Gayle?"

Not six feet below them now, the glowing orbs blinked slowly, once, twice, then moved slightly, and suddenly Eve knew beyond all doubt that they were eyes and they were looking right at her. "Run!" she screamed, dragging Sam with her. She glimpsed Merilynn bringing up the rear just as the banshee shriek spiraled up behind them, so loud and ragged that it hurt her ears.

The rain pelted her face, but Eve didn't notice, and each time any one of the girls tripped, the other two would scoop the third to her feet, barely missing a stride. Soaked with rain, legs sheathed in mud and leaves, they skidded the last few feet down the hillside to the rowboat and, wordless, pushed it into the water, turning it around as soon as it was afloat. They climbed in, Eve and Sam both grabbing oars and sitting so that they faced the land across the lake. They began paddling, and Eve quickly copied Sam's sure, deep strokes that moved them rapidly away from the island despite the wind. The banshee shriek receded, mingling with the howls of the storm. Thunder cracked.

Merilynn sat in the prow, facing the island, her green gaze dark and unwavering. Even a flash of lightning didn't spark them.

"What do you see?" Sam asked when they were a quarter of the way across the lake.

Merilynn squinted toward Applehead Island. Rain swatted the onyx surface, oars sluiced up freshets of lake water to mix and fall back down with the rain. "I don't know," she said after a long moment. "I don't know what I saw."

Steadily, they continued to row. To Eve, Merilynn looked like a solemn lady in a medieval painting. Beside her, Sam sat straight, her chin set, her entire profile showing determination. Eve copied her, and although her arms were beginning to ache, she didn't complain at all, but just kept rowing. It was almost as dark as night, the forest swathed in dark green-grays. Once, she looked down at the water, watching it move under the oars and, deep, deep below, thought she saw little lights winking on. Yellow-white and dim, like the lights of a town glimpsed from an airplane window on a stormy night.

"Something wrong, Evie?" Sam asked as she rowed.

"No." Telling herself it was only reflected lightning, Eve kept her eyes on the shoreline because she knew that if she looked down and the lights were still there, she'd start screaming and wouldn't be able to stop.

Today

3

Eve Camlan, dressed only in her pink cotton baby-doll pj's, the ones with the little white rabbits printed all over them, fought down the urge to huddle up and try to keep her bunnies hidden. She hadn't even had a robe handy when the rush committee from Gamma Eta Pi pounded on her dorm room door and snatched her from her bed. Most of the other girls sitting on the sofas and chairs in the big, high-ceilinged common room of Gamma House had chosen their sleepwear with the rush in mind. They wore neat satin pajamas or long silky nightgowns with matching robes. A few wore sleep T-shirts, the shortest still providing more leg coverage than Eve's idiotic bunny outfit.

Some of the girls even looked like they'd gone to bed with lipstick on, just in case. At least there weren't many positive fashion statements in the hair department; evidently no one had managed to grab a brush as they were pulled out of their doors. Eve's hair was pulled back in a low ponytail and now she reached up and removed the pink scrunchie. Slipping it onto her wrist like a bracelet, she quickly combed her fingers through the golden mane, encouraging the natural curls to spring to life. *Thank heaven for the waves.* When she was younger, she straightened it most days, but now she knew the loose waves she'd inherited from her mother let her look fashionably tousled when straight-haired girls looked as if they had limp spaghetti stuck on their heads.

Still, she wished she had a robe, a mirror, and some lipstick. *Look confident,* she reminded herself. Looking confident was the key to everything. She'd learned that years and years ago, back in the cheerleader camp run by sisters of this very sorority to which she hoped to pledge. She'd really learned about confidence more from Samantha Penrose than the college-age counselors, but that was beside the point. *I'm sitting here in pink rabbit baby-dolls, waiting to be judged worthy of the best house on campus. The only house if I really want to be a cheerleader. The only house I ever wanted to join. Stupid, stupid, stupid!*

And she'd wanted to get into Gamma since that first summer at cheerleader camp. At the end of her ninth summer, she'd gone back to school and practiced on her own, then returned to the camp to learn more, back and forth, two more summers, until she reached junior high, aced the tryouts, and made the cheerleading squad. She'd soon made captain, then, in high school, been chosen for the varsity squad on her first try. She worked her way up to second-in-command of the squad and prom queen in her junior year, and in her senior, she was captain *and* homecoming queen. And in the annual, she was voted Most Likely to Be a Movie Star, which gave her a little thrill even though she didn't want to be a movie star. That year she graduated with honors after *lots* of hard studying and was accepted to Greenbriar University, even garnering a small scholarship, which added to the college fund her parents had saved for her. She could study and practice cheering full-time without having to flip burgers. She would have time to do volunteer work too, but she hadn't started yet. School had barely begun and she wanted to volunteer for one of the Gamma charities if she got in. *I'm in. They wouldn't have rushed me tonight if I wasn't in.* . . .

Still, she had doubts, which was silly, since she had accomplished everything she'd set out to do in her life so far. Next on her list was this—being accepted as a sister of Gamma Eta Pi, making the varsity cheerleader squad, eventually becoming captain and the president of the sorority, and finding true love along the way. She'd never thought out her plans for after college since it seemed so far away, but if her true love hadn't yet appeared, maybe she'd tryout to be a cheerleader for a pro football team. She had the figure for it even if she wasn't as tall as most of the pros. Or maybe she'd become a junior high school teacher and coach the beginning cheerleading squad for the school. Or, if her true love happened to be well-to-do or good at making money, she wouldn't have to work for other people at all. Maybe she could start her own cheerleading school. She smiled to herself, liking the idea. A lot.

"Hi, I'm Kendra," said the girl next to her on the overstuffed cabbage-rose-covered sofa. Her sparkling smile was infectious.

Eve smiled back, wishing she'd popped a breath mint. "Hi. I'm Eve Camlan. Aren't you in Professor Piccolo's English 101 with me?"

"Eleven A.M.? Yeah. That's where I thought I recognized you from. I hate those stupid journals we're supposed to keep, don't you?"

"Yeah. Like I'm going to tell some ancient guy in his forties my private thoughts."

"I know, isn't that disgusting to even *think* about?"

Eve laughed softly. "You know what I do? I look up the soap opera plots for the week in *TV Guide*, and write down things I see there like it's from my life. You know, 'I think my aunt is having an affair with her husband's brother's uncle,' or 'I think the mailman may be the real father of my neighbors' new baby.'"

"Mr. Mailman's making deliveries, huh?" Kendra chuckled warmly. "I love it. Do you want to know what I do?"

"Yes. What?"

"Pretty much the same thing, only worse."

"What do you mean?"

"I make up rumors about students for him."

"Who?"

She laughed again. "Don't worry, not about anybody real. I say stuff about how I was way deep in the library stacks and saw a couple doing the dirty on the floor in front of the paleontology books."

"I saw that on *Friends.*"

"Me too." Kendra beamed at her. "See? We're doing the same thing. When I can't think of anything, I turn on *The Brady Bunch* and tell some story from Marcia's—I mean *my*—childhood."

"That's more fun than what I do. You're so creative!"

"Well, I don't know about that. I just take modern folklore and spice it up a little more. You could too." She snickered. "You should say you saw the couple in the anthropology stacks too. I bet Piccolo would start hanging around there to see if it's true. I bet he likes to watch!"

"You're bad," Eve said happily.

"Thanks. And isn't *this* exciting?" Kendra nodded toward the other side of the room where the rush committee, wearing daytime clothes, sat huddled together around an ornate antique desk, conferring.

"Yes. I wish I'd dressed better."

Kendra, in a black satin pajama set—shorts and

a short-sleeved button-down top, both trimmed with neat bronze piping—checked her out. "You look fine."

"I feel naked."

"Why? You wearing crotchless panties or something?"

Eve burst into restrained giggles. "No, of course not."

"Well, you don't look naked to me. Can't see a thing through those bunnies."

Eve rolled her eyes. "These make me look like I'm ten years old. I have nice pajamas, but I got superstitious and thought that if I put them on, I wouldn't be chosen." She felt her cheeks heat up. "You know what I mean? Pretty stupid, huh?"

"I know. It's silly, but not stupid. My granny's like that. She throws salt over her shoulder and won't walk under ladders."

"Oh, well, I'm not that bad. Not that that's bad—I mean—"

"Oh, hush up," the dark-haired girl said, smiling. "That's okay. I know what you mean. My granny isn't totally superstitious; she's not afraid of black cats. She has one named Luthor and he crosses her path all the time. He's got the biggest green eyes you ever saw. Sometimes, the way he stares at you, I think he should be named Lucifer, not Luthor." She paused. "What's wrong? You afraid of cats?"

"No, I love cats," Eve said. "I love all animals."

"Well, you look like somebody just walked over

your grave." Another brilliant grin. "At least that's what my granny would say."

"The thing you said about big green eyes made me remember once, when I was little, seeing green eyes glowing in a cave. It was a mountain lion, I think. It scared me half to death. Sometimes I still have nightmares."

"A mountain lion?"

Eve nodded.

"But you don't *know* it was a mountain lion? You just *think* it was?"

"My friends and I ran." That stormy afternoon on the island didn't come back to her very often—she didn't allow it—but when it did, she felt as if it were happening all over again. "One of the girls I was with, this kind of brainiac tomboy, she said it had to be a mountain lion."

"Wow. Where'd that happen?"

Eve clasped her hands together to stop a tremble from coming on. "You know Applehead Lake?"

"Sure. It's like, what, a mile's walk through the woods behind the campus?"

"Yeah. We were at the cheerleader camp on the far side of the lake. We stole a boat and rowed out to the island. That's where we saw it. The mountain lion. A storm was coming up and the wind was howling and we scared ourselves half to death."

"You've gone all white on white," Kendra said, touching her hand. "It's still scary for you, isn't it?"

"A little, I guess."

"Have you ever heard the stories about the green ghost or the Forest Knight? They're really the same thing."

Eve's smile was wry. "Yes. The other girl I was with thought that's what we saw. She didn't think it was a mountain lion. She said it was either the green ghost or Holly Gayle. Do you know about her?"

"Who doesn't?" Kendra said. "That girl's supposed to haunt *this* house."

Eve glanced around the room, taking in everything from the crystal vases of fresh roses to the ornate molding on the high ceilings, the dark wainscoting, and the floral wallpaper, heavy forest green blotched with big reddish roses trailing ivy. The room was filled with roses in every form. She could smell them, a cloying sweetness that seemed old and stale, not fresh. She glanced at the cabbage rose slipcovers. Way too many roses, and it made the room spooky and Gothic-looking. "Holly haunts this house? Back at camp, I heard she was trapped under the lake. It involved some sort of story about treasure and sacrifices. Silly kid stuff."

"My granny's granny worked here when Holly Gayle disappeared in 1909. She was a cleaning lady, right here in this very house, from the time she was just fourteen years old. And Holly Gayle was a sorority sister." Kendra leaned closer and whispered, "Part of the secret sorority."

"Secret sorority?"

"Shh. You don't know about that?"

Eve shook her head.

"Don't ask. I'll tell you later, when we're not here. Anyway, listen. Holly disappeared and they said she killed herself or was murdered, drowned in the lake. Granny's granny said she saw her ghost walking along the lake shore once, and that she looked real at first, but then just sort of faded away. Later, they started seeing her walking around in the house sometimes. Maybe they still do."

"They never found her body?"

Kendra shook her head. "Never."

Eve hid her nervousness. "Maybe she just ran away. Maybe she wasn't killed on purpose and maybe she didn't commit suicide. Maybe she eloped. Maybe she fell in love with some prince and went to Europe to live in a castle. Or maybe she wanted to go to New York and be an actress. Maybe—"

"No," Kendra said firmly. "Granny's granny recognized her."

"But how did she know she died in the lake?"

"That's easy, girl. She wore this old-fashioned long white dress and it was soaking wet from her being drowned. And sometimes, even when Granny's granny couldn't see her, she *smelled* her. Granny's mama saw her once, too, and smelled her lots of times. She said she heard her scream-ing and crying a few times. And Granny even saw her *and* smelled her, both, just once, when she went in one of the rooms upstairs. Holly's ghost was in there, looking out the window. Granny thought she was a student and said hello, and the girl turned and Granny saw her eyes even though the room was pretty dark. And then she just faded away and Granny heard a scream as this big old whoosh of wind passed over her. She smelled the smell and Granny knew it was the ghost. She said it was the devil's business, and she left and never came back. She said the smell scared her more than her eyes, and the eyes *glowed. Green.* "

"Perfume?" Eve asked, purposely ignoring the part about the green eyes. "I've heard stories about ghosts who trail perfume in old castles in England and Scotland."

"You've got castles on the brain. And, no, it wasn't perfume. She smelled like the lake. You know that smell. That cold, dark, watery smell."

"Yes, I know that smell." She paused, pushing away memories, getting herself together. "Was your granny a student here?"

Kendra laughed lightly. "Are you serious or are you just trying to be politically correct?"

"I'm serious."

Kendra studied her, then smiled. "No, but when she was a girl, she worked here for a while, with her mama. *My* mama was the first woman in our family to go to college."

"Here?"

"No. Granny wouldn't let her. She said this was a bad place. Mama went to Cal Poly in San Luis Obispo."

"So why are you here?"

"Because I wanted to go here in honor of all the people in my family who worked at Greenbriar over the years." She grinned. "And I wanted to join Gamma House because this is where my three grannies worked."

"What does your granny think of you going here?"

"She tried to talk me out of it. Said if I had to come here, to stay away from this house. Said it was evil. Isn't that funny?"

"Um, is it? I mean, she must hate that you're here at Gamma. What did she say when you told her you wanted to pledge?"

"You kidding? I didn't tell her."

"What about your mother? Does she know?"

Kendra's smile faded. "Not exactly. I told her I'm thinking about it. She doesn't want me to, not really, but she's conflicted, too. You know, she thinks Granny's silly about the ghost stories, but she's not so sure about some of the other stuff."

"What other stuff?"

"Hush." Kendra glanced around, then bent closer to Eve. "The secret stuff. I'll tell you later." She relaxed. "My mom's good about my coming to Greenbriar for my degree. She kinda likes it, in fact. She couldn't afford to rebel and

come here, so I'm doing it for her, you know?"
She tilted her head. "So, why did *you* choose
Greenbriar?"

"Cheerleading camp. The counselors were
cheerleaders from Gamma."

"You're kidding."

"No. Why would you think that?"

"This is West Coast Ivy League. People come
here for the name 'Greenbriar' on their diplomas.
So, come on, what's your major?"

Eve flushed, suddenly ashamed. "I haven't
declared yet."

Kendra patted her hand. "Lots of people don't
choose for a couple years. You've got plenty of
time."

"What's your major?"

"Sociology or anthropology or psychology. I
don't know, exactly. I want to study cultures and
folklore, you know, do the Joseph Campbell
thing."

Eve grinned. "So part of the reason you want to
be in Gamma is to check out the ghost stories?"

Kendra studied her nails briefly. "Of course,
but I didn't tell my family."

"You aren't afraid of ghosts?"

"No. They're just stories."

"Come on. If you thought that, you wouldn't
be here looking for them."

Kendra shrugged, one side of her mouth
crooked up. "See? I knew you were too smart to
just be a pom-pom girl. I've seen a few strange

things, but they're nothing to be frightened of. The stories are scarier than reality."

"What—"

Two sharp hand claps interrupted Eve's question.

4

"May I have your attention, please?"

Eve looked up at the exotic raven-haired young woman who now stood before the huge fireplace at the end of the room. The hearth was dark this warm September night. Instead of fire, between the andirons lay—what else?—a huge spray of dried roses, their tints faded false flames of apricot, red, and yellow.

"I'm Malory Thomas, president of Gamma Eta Pi."

Her teeth flashed brilliant and white as her dark eyes flickered over the pajama-clad girls in the room. Briefly, she caught Eve's gaze and held it. Eve tried to smile back, but her lip barely trembled before the eyes moved on to their next target. She had met Malory on rush night and had been just as intimidated by her then as now. The Gamma president, with her regal bearing, implacable features, and milk-white skin, was an ice goddess, maybe the Snow Queen herself. Eve glanced at Kendra, who replied with a hint of a smile. Eve felt better;

she could tell that Kendra didn't like Malory either.

"Welcome," Malory continued. "As I'm sure you all suspect, you have been selected as pledges for Gamma Eta Pi, the oldest, most prestigious sorority on Greenbriar's campus. In fact, Gamma maintains chapters at the most exclusive universities not only nationwide, but around the world. Our sisterhood is small but it is the best."

She paused, letting her eyes graze the room. "You have rigorous times ahead of you, pledges, in order to prove yourselves worthy of Gamma. Some of you won't make it—in fact, probably fewer than half of you will."

The room seemed to chill ten degrees. Eve hugged herself.

"All of you will be required to swear an oath never to repeat what you see or hear in this house, whether you make it to full sisterhood or not."

Someone cleared her throat. Malory turned toward the sound. "Do you have a question?"

"No," a Chinese girl said softly. She looked embarrassed. "I just had a frog in my—"

"Throat," Malory finished briskly. "Are you *sure* you don't have a question?"

"Yes."

"Maybe you're just a little nervous? You don't need to be nervous. You may ask whatever you wish."

The girl shook her head. "No questions."

"I have a question," Kendra said.

Eve tried to disappear as Malory turned in their direction. "Yes? And you are?"

"Kendra Phillips."

"What's your question, Kendra?"

"Say a pledge washes out and then she talks about what happens here. What will happen to her?"

Malory smiled with her mouth but not her eyes, nodding as she glanced around to include the other pledges in her answer. "Congratulations, Kendra. I'm sure all your sisters-to-be are wondering the same thing, but none of them had the courage to ask."

Casting withering glances at the new girls, she paced the length of the room, from the fireplace to the room entrance. The double doors were wide open, and beyond the room the large foyer twinkled with quavery light cast from a crystal chandelier Eve had admired the first time she visited the house.

"I can't tell you what will happen to a pledge who breaks her vows until you take the vows," Malory said, moving toward the center of the room again. "But I can tell you that those who have broken them generally end up leaving Greenbriar University and won't be welcomed at any other learning institution where a Gamma chapter exists." She approached Kendra. "Does that answer your question?"

Kendra met her gaze. "I guess it does. Thank you."

Malory addressed the room. "Any of you who wish to, may leave now or after this meeting without any repercussions. If you are uncomfortable with the idea of secrecy within our sisterhood or feel that you can't maintain our trust, we ask that you not return.

"Those of you who wish to proceed with pledging are asked to return to the house tomorrow afternoon between three and six o'clock to sign in as official pledges. After six, we will convene to get better acquainted and begin your initiations into the sisterhood."

A girl sitting on a pillow on the floor almost out of Eve's view raised her hand. Eve craned her head to see her, but only saw some long red hair and the sleeve of a forest-green pajama top.

"Yes?" said Malory.

"Are initiations allowed?" the young woman asked quickly.

She sounded familiar to Eve, but Malory laughed. "Of course initiations are allowed. Miss?"

"Morris."

Morris, thought Eve. *It couldn't be . . .*

"Miss Morris, I think you're referring to hazings." She looked around the room. "Hazings are beneath us and, no, *they* aren't allowed. You all know what hazings are, don't you?"

No one replied, though a general murmur arose.

"Fraternities, especially jock fraternities, are notorious for hazing, a practice long banned here at Greenbriar. Years ago, however, one of the fraternities here routinely stripped their pledges, blindfolded them, and took them out on Applehead Lake, then dropped them from a rowboat into the water. They did this at night, during the dark of the moon so when a pledge tore his blindfold off, he still couldn't see where he was. He had to swim to shore. If he couldn't make it—if the brothers in the boat had to rescue him—he was rejected. The practice ended in 1972, when a pledge drowned." She paced back to the fireplace. "You will be put to the test, ladies, no doubt about that. But we will not humiliate you in public. You have my promise of that."

Eve wondered if they would humiliate her in private instead. *Stop thinking like that. The other sisters look nice. And there's nothing wrong with Malory. She's just not your kind of person.* She watched Malory turn and nod at the Gamma sisters seated at the desk. Two of them rose and came to join her in front of the fireplace.

"This is our rush chairman, Heather Horner." Malory indicated the girl to her right. She had curly shoulder-length chestnut hair and when she smiled her eyes crinkled with humor. Eve instantly decided she liked her. "If you decide to go ahead with your pledging, Heather will be at the desk tomorrow afternoon with the papers for you to sign."

"Excuse me," Eve heard herself say.

"Yes?" Malory answered. "You are?"

"Eve—Genevieve Camlan. Are the papers we sign tomorrow our oaths?" *God, I sound so stupid!* "I mean, is that all there is to becoming a pledge?" *Kill me now. Just kill me now!*

Heather answered in a warm voice. "The papers just make you an official pledge."

"And as an official pledge, you are sworn to forever keep the secrets of our sisterhood," Malory added darkly, "whether you make it into full sisterhood or not."

"Th-thank you."

Cocking an eyebrow, Malory gestured at the sister on her left, a shiny blonde in a short scoop-necked top and designer jeans. She had a small yellow bag of Peanut M&Ms in her hand and appeared to have one or two of the candies stuffed in one cheek. A belly button ring glittered gold against her stomach and Eve spied part of a small tattoo of a red rose blooming on her left hipbone, just above her jeans. "This is the sorority's vice president, Brittany Woodcock."

"Hi, pledges!" she chirped, then popped another M&M in her glossy-painted mouth and crunched.

Kendra stifled a giggle. Eve elbowed her but didn't look her way, knowing that if they made eye contact, she'd laugh too. Vice President Brittany sounded like a dumb blond chipmunk.

"Welcome to Gamma Eta Pi House," she chirped. "From the looks of some of you, it'll be

Gamma Eta *Cherry* Pi House! How many of you are virgins?"

Only Malory's glacial glare silenced the unesteemed vice president, who blinked and backed up a step as the president spoke. "Attention, please, everyone. Still seated at the desk are our other senior officers, Treasurer Michele Marano and Secretary Teri Knolls."

The duo nodded greetings. They were both attractive, but not particularly memorable; Eve wasn't sure if they'd actually talked before.

"The tradition of the sisters of Gamma is long and distinguished," Malory continued. "If you become one of us, you will be among the most powerful women on earth. You will share your lives with your sisters, now and forever. You will always have friends. You will have the best careers in whatever fields you choose. As long as you have your sisters, you will never have enemies— or if you do, you won't have to worry about them. As sisters, and later as alumni of Gamma Eta Pi, you will help change the world." She flashed her predatory smile. "Any questions?"

There weren't.

"Go back to your beds now and think about your decision. It may be the most important one of your life. We hope to see you tomorrow afternoon. Good night."

Malory Thomas turned on her heel and walked briskly toward the side of the room, Brittany right behind her. Just as Eve started to look forward to her slamming into the wall, a panel slid open. They disappeared into darkness.

The panel slid closed again so quickly and silently that Eve almost wondered if she had really seen the opening at all.

The two sisters manning the desk, Michele and Teri, rose and left the room the old-fashioned way—through the open doors—but not one of the pajama-clad pledges made a move. Heather Horner, still standing before the fireplace, grinned. "Our president has a flair for drama, kids," she said, walking forward. "See you all tomorrow!"

The pledges responded this time, getting up and leaving singly and in groups of two or three. As Eve and Kendra stood up, Heather said, "Eve? Just a minute."

Eve turned, surprised. "Yes?"

Heather smiled and crooked her finger. Eve stepped forward while Kendra hung back.

"I'm the captain of the varsity cheerleading team," Heather told her. "I hope you're intending to join the squad."

Eve beamed. "Well, I sure want to try out!"

"Trying out is just a formality for you. If you want it, you're in, as long as you pledge the sorority. You *are* pledging, right?"

"Yes!" All lingering doubts fled in that instant.

The girl smiled warmly. "You've got so many awards, you're like the star quarterback all the colleges want for their team. We want you for our squad!"

"I—thanks, but I just have a few little high school awards," Eve began, but she couldn't stand pretending to be humble and bubbled, "And it's why I came here! I want to be on your squad more than anything!"

Heather laughed, then leaned forward and hugged her. "I know. I read your letter and your recommendations from your high school coach. Welcome to the squad," she said softly. "To keep it fair, we can't just announce you're already in, you know—"

"I know. Thank you so much for telling me, though!"

"Is your friend trying out?" Heather glanced Kendra's way.

"My friend? Oh, I don't know. We just met. I don't think so, though. Why?"

"I just wondered. I think this should be our little secret for now, either way."

"Sure." She started to reach for Heather's hand, but the other girl bypassed it and gave her a warm hug instead. "Welcome, Sister."

Eve just grinned.

5

Eve and Kendra walked out of Gamma House together, and neither spoke until they were well away from the huge old southern-style mansion. "A transplanted plantation house," Eve observed.

"Sure is," Kendra murmured as they continued to walk. "Kind of creepy."

The house was set far back on a long greensward, Applehead Forest dark behind it. Before it, the wide veranda met the low stairway down to an elderly cracked sidewalk edged with rosebushes. It led straight across twenty yards of manicured lawn before reaching a long rectangular reflecting pool where it divided into two walkways, one leading along either side of the pool. Unseen frogs croaked on dark lily pads floating in patches on the still water.

"All this place needs is some moss hanging from the trees and fireflies blinking around, and I'd think we were at Tara with Rhett and Scarlett."

"Don't forget the kudzu vine and big-ass mosquitoes," Kendra said.

"You've been there?"

"My father's family still lives down there. Sometimes we'd visit during summer vacation. Trust me, it's a lot nicer here." Kendra stopped walking and glanced back at the mansion. "I'm not too sure I want to live in that old house."

"Why? It's so big and beautiful and cool!"

Kendra chuckled. "You're really stoked about this place, aren't you?"

"Yes!"

"It doesn't spook you or give you any funny feelings?"

"You mean because of the ghost stories?"

Kendra shrugged.

"Of course not. I don't believe in ghosts." Eve shivered despite her words and the late summer heat, imagining green eyes glowing out at her from the forest behind the house. "Let's go. I've got early classes."

They reached the road and crossed it, then followed a much newer walkway across the campus, past darkened Gothic buildings and up through a tree-filled garden area, finally arriving at their dorm rooms, which turned out to be located on different floors of the same big square building. The faceless multistoried dormitory looked like it had been built in the sixties or seventies and much of its unadorned ugliness was blessedly hidden by pines and oaks. The dorm didn't fit in with the older main buildings of the college any more than the

Gamma's plantation house did. The whole campus was, Eve thought, a decorator's nightmare.

Even at midnight, the September air was warm enough that Eve didn't feel chilled in her horrible rabbit nightie. "Kendra?" she asked as the other girl reached for the glass door to let them into the building.

"Yes?"

"That secret stuff you were talking about. When will you tell me about it?"

Kendra studied her. "I don't know if I should. Judging by the hug you got, I think maybe you're on the fast track right into the secret stuff."

"That wasn't anything." Eve grinned. "Don't tell, but I think I'm in the varsity cheerleading squad. Heather's the captain."

"Well . . ." Kendra paused as a girl in forest green pajamas and a matching robe approached. "Hi."

"Hi." The girl smiled. She had beautiful long straight red hair and eyes so green that even in the bad light, they shone.

Oh, my God. "Hi," Eve managed. *It* is *her.*

"Have we met?" the redhead asked.

"Uh, I don't think so."

"You look familiar. What's your name?"

"Eve."

"Right. You asked a question at the meeting. I think we've met somewhere before. You look familiar and your name fits you. I mean, if I had to guess your name, I'd guess Eve."

"Maybe you met at the rush party," Kendra said, watching the two of them.

"I'm Merilynn Morris. Do you recognize my name?" She pinned Eve with her eyes.

"I—I'm not sure. Maybe. You said it at the meeting. That's probably why it sounds a little familiar."

Merilynn gazed at her steadily. "That must be it. Well, good night." She pushed open the door and disappeared inside.

"What was all that about?" Kendra asked.

"Nothing."

"You want me to tell you the secret stuff, you don't lie to me. What was that? Where do you know her from?"

"You know the mountain lion story from when I was a kid at cheer camp?"

"Yes."

"She was one of the girls I was with."

Kendra considered. "So what's the problem? Why didn't you say so?"

"I don't know." She looked at Kendra and shrugged. "I really don't know."

"Come on." Kendra opened the door and held it for her. "We'll talk later. Let's get some sleep."

6

Professor Piccolo's English 101 class was filled to bursting with young women, and young women were exactly what the good professor loved most. They came in all shapes and sizes, in all colors and fragrances, and with nary an exception, Timothy Piccolo worshipped them all.

Women were his reason for being, his sum, his all. He lived for the scent of a woman's skin, for the silky touch of feminine flesh. He knew the soft warm fragrance of the nape of a woman's neck that had been hidden beneath a curtain of long hair, and eyes closed, he could tell the scent of the back of a feminine knee from that of an elbow. He could tell a delicate blonde from a luxurious brunette and could identify the special spice of a redhead.

Piccolo looked across the sea of young women and as he spoke of Shakespeare and Bacon, he studied a slender gamine and thought of the taste of her lightly freckled sun-warmed skin. He drank in the beauty of a feminine Othello in the first row, her long legs stretching endlessly from nearly-not-there sandals and enameled maroon toenails to the shadowed triangle under her desk. He couldn't tell if she wore a skirt or shorts, but it didn't matter; in his mind, his face was buried in that triangle, nose inhaling, tongue exploring the treasures folded within. Musk, he thought, and spice. *A hint of cinnamon? Perhaps.*

A fresh-faced blonde sat at the desk next to the lady Moor's and he saw them exchange glances as he spoke. *Ah, to be the meat in that sandwich.* He had noticed them both before, just as he noticed all women, but had never seen any sign that they knew one another until now. The pairing excited him. The blonde was a blushing peach, but a California peach, not a Georgian. An all-American girl full of enthusiasm and bouncy friendliness. He could tell these things by looks and body language without ever hearing her speak. She was a true blonde with unblemished clear skin and thick waves of golden hair grazing her collarbone. Nordic-blue eyes gazed at him from above perfect lips painted a delicate shade of pink. Her fingernail enamel matched her lipstick, but her toes were a mystery, hidden in bright white Reeboks and short pink socks.

Her denim cutoffs were short, but not too short; she gave off innocent sexuality, sun-kissed fruit hanging ripe and ready to be plucked. Her legs were very lightly tanned, as were her arms. She wore a pale pink and blue plaid camp shirt open over a light blue tank top that revealed a luscious hint of cleavage. He spoke of blank verse as he imagined being smothered between those perfect globes. If he were to move forward now and kneel to gently roll up her tank top to reveal her breasts, he knew he would find nipples the color of pink roses and, if he were to oh-so-carefully cup one breast and lift it so that his tongue could taste the sweat beneath it, he knew he would die of pleasure.

A giggle startled him. A soft musical giggle, just two syllables. Another, a trio of titters, followed from somewhere else in the classroom and Timothy Piccolo realized his participle was no longer dangling. Quickly, he moved behind his desk and continued his lecture, his eyes alighting briefly on girl after girl, passing over the males as if they didn't exist.

Eyes of all colors returned his looks, most of them smiling eyes. A few lips were licked and, unable to resist, he paused and picked up his bottle of Evian. Unscrewing the lid, he said, "Any questions?" then drank.

For just an instant, he allowed his tongue to lave the bottle's opening. He flipped a water drop onto his upper lip as he lowered the bottle and reattached the lid. Then his tongue, a snake wishing to hide in bush, flickered out and cleaned the stray drop of water away.

The proverbial pin might have dropped in that bare instant; if it had it would have been as loud as a rock smashing into a wall. They were watching him. They had heard about his tongue. His wonderful, talented tongue.

Fresh giggles interrupted the silence. Professor Tongue cleared his throat and returned to his lecture.

Few of his admirers ever met his tongue, for he was a man of honor, and did not allow himself to indulge in any relations with students under twenty-one. In fact, he never touched less than a senior and really preferred graduate students. There were female teachers and professors who tempted him almost daily, but he rarely allowed himself to be seduced since he knew from experience that jealousies among the ladies were inevitable. That was the joy of the senior student: she would graduate and be off instead of becoming a problem. And, as an instructor, he always hoped that each of his loves would teach her future beaus a little about the art of the tongue. They were all wonderful girls, wonderful women, and they deserved the best.

Professor Piccolo smiled at the class, ending his lecture so that the bell rang as a coda. He beamed from his desk as a handful of young ladies rushed up with trumped-up excuses to talk to him, to flirt, to test the waters. To perhaps see him lick his lips. They loved to see his tongue—

it was a legend in his own mouth. A warm tingly feeling shot through his groin. There was a reason his egghead buddies called him the Cunning Linguist.

7

Eve and Kendra sat on an ornate wooden bench in the shade of a gnarled oak on a broad lawn dotted with other lunching students. Both starving, they'd bought take-out food from the student cafeteria and now, unwrapping it, they looked at each other and giggled. Well, Eve giggled. Kendra was more the sophisticated chuckle type. The type, Eve knew, that rarely had any interest in cheerleaders.

"What?" Kendra opened a container of not-quite-fresh-looking fresh fruit chunks and stuck two forks in unidentifiable orange-colored pieces. "What do you think these are? Peaches or mangos? And what are you looking at me like that for?"

Eve took the speared fruit and popped it in her mouth, chewed, and swallowed. "Mango. Probably. It's hard to tell. Whatever it is, it's not awful."

Kendra tried a piece, then went back for a chunk of pineapple. "Now, tell me about that look you were giving me."

"'Well, in high school, girls like you didn't usually like girls like me."

"What? Explain that a little more."

"Well, you're into studying."

"You think I'm a nerd?"

"No! No! That's not what I meant. Nerds don't look like you do. They don't know how to dress or do their hair. They don't even care, most of the time."

Kendra chuckled and handed Eve half of a chicken salad sandwich. "I don't care like you do. You look so perfect, it's hard to tell you have makeup on, but you do."

"Sure."

"I'm not wearing any."

"I could show you—"

"No. I know how." Kendra grinned. "Like you said, I'm not a nerd. I'm just not into doing all that primping if I don't have to."

"That's what I mean," Eve said, pointing the corner of her sandwich at the other girl. "You're sort of beyond it all. I mean, you're smart and beautiful, and you don't care about cheerleading, right?"

"No, I don't care about cheerleading. I've noticed a few football players that look like they're worth cheering, though. This chicken salad doesn't have any celery in it. That's not right."

"It isn't?"

"Nope. I think I'll complain."

"Really? It's just a sandwich."

"Maybe they'll put celery in it if I complain—
that means ask nicely. They sure won't if I don't
say anything."

"See? That's what I mean. You think things
through. You're, um, mature. You were probably
born mature."

Kendra laughed. "Thanks, I think. And what
about you? Were you born to be perky?"

Eve hesitated. "Usually, if a girl like you asked
me that, I'd know I was being put down. I don't
think you're doing that though. Are you?"

"Of course not. So, were you born perky or did
you learn it?"

"I don't know. A little bit of both, probably. My
mother was a beauty queen. She started in
pageants when she was eight years old." Eve shook
her head. "She was Little Miss Annie's Baton
School, Little Miss Caledonia, Miss Caledonia
Dairy Products, and even Miss Central California.
She always did flaming batons, and boy, was she
good!" Eve giggled. "Sometimes, if she has too
much to drink at Christmas, she wants to do her
old act, but Daddy always stops her because he's
afraid she'll catch herself on fire."

"That's nice."

"Huh?"

"He worries that *she'll* catch on fire, not that
the house will. So do you do beauty pageants?"

"She kind of tried to get me to, but I didn't
like it. I only did one, when I was little, and she
stopped trying to get me to do any more after

that little girl was murdered in Colorado and the news started doing exposés on kid pageants."

"So how are you with flaming batons?"

Eve had a long sip of Diet Coke. "Fire scares me. Daddy said that once, when I was about two, my mother had too much eggnog and managed to get her batons lit before he could stop her. I kind of remember, but not really. She threw the batons up and they hit the ceiling, of course, and came down hard. He said one landed a foot from me and that I just stood there and stared at it and wouldn't talk for a couple days. I had nightmares for a long time."

"About the batons?"

"Yeah, but not exactly. I kept dreaming that clouds would gather for a storm and then instead of water, it would rain drops of fire." She didn't add that the dreams only went away after the incident at Applehead Lake, to be replaced by nightmares about glowing green eyes and black lake water pounded by real rain.

"So, was your mother a cheerleader?"

"A twirler." Eve made her voice as serious as she could. "Me, I'm a pom-pom woman."

It worked. Kendra snorted laughter. "How'd they meet? Your parents, I mean?"

"Mom was Miss Central Coast. Daddy was one of the judges." She cocked an eyebrow. "And it's not what you're probably thinking. No funny business—Hi, Heather!"

"Hi, you two!" The captain of the cheerleading

squad approached quickly, chestnut curls bounc-
ing in the sun. She wore a short-skirted cheering
uniform, green trimmed in gold and white. It
was gorgeous. Even more gorgeous with the pair
of guys flanking her. They were big, clean-cut
young men, one light, one dark, both with
gleaming smiles. They weren't in uniform, but
Eve knew they were football players.

"I want you to meet Art Caliburn and Spencer
Lake. Art is the Knights' captain and star quarterback, and Spence is a wide receiver." Heather
smiled. "They're both being scouted by the
majors."

The blond stepped forward and extended his
hand. "I'm Art."

Kendra took it and introduced herself; then
Eve did the same. She could feel herself blushing
as the hunky football player looked into her eyes.
Sparks seemed to tingle between their hands.
Then Spence stepped in, speaking first to
Kendra, then breaking the grip between Art and
Eve, replacing the QB's hand with his own.

More sparks flew. Maybe even bigger sparks.

"Can't wait to see you two cheering on our
team," Art said, breaking the spell.

Kendra laughingly declined but Eve just kept
blushing. College was going to be even more fun
than she'd expected.

8

Signing the pledge agreement had been anti-climactic, to say the least. Now Eve dawdled in the big main room of the house, studying old paintings, old wallpaper, and various antiques. The room smelled old, centuries old, and roses, fresh and dried lay above the ancient background scent, like flowers in a mausoleum.

She wanted to check out the house, but nobody else seemed to be taking self-guided tours. If Kendra showed up soon, maybe they could take a look around together. She glanced at her watch; it was only a little after four o'clock and not too many pledges or sisters were here yet. Heather was the only person she knew, and she was busy at the sign-up table doing her thing as rush chairman. Her Majesty Malory had yet to make an appearance and that was half the reason Eve didn't want to go wandering by herself—she might run into her.

She walked out into the huge foyer. The floor was covered with white marble tile streaked in browns ranging from tan to russet. Sheer curtains covered tall narrow sidelights on each side of the door, the thick old glass casting odd prisms across the floor. The distance from the front entrance to the central grand staircase was about twice the width of her small dorm room. It was breathtaking. The broad staircase went up a dozen steps, then swept into two separate normal-width stairways, one to the west wing, one to the east. They disappeared from view at the first-floor landing, which appeared to run along the length of the old mansion. As she watched, Eve heard a door above open and close. Feminine voices echoed from above and two of the sisters came into view. They saw her staring at them.

"Hello!" Eve said with all the cheer she could muster.

"Hi," said one, an Asian girl with blond streaks in her hair. The other girl, pale with smooth glossy dark hair curling under an inch below her firm jawline, looked at her and nodded, then looked again.

Eve didn't like the look, though it wasn't mean or cold. It was just curious. "Have we met?" the girl asked.

It can't be Sam Penrose. She'd never join a sorority. Or wear makeup. Or a dress. Never a dress. "I don't think so. Maybe at the rush party?"

The girl—*it's not Sam Penrose, I haven't seen her since camp, she's just the same type*—opened her mouth to say something, then paused, looking behind Eve. Eve turned to see one of the entrance doors opening. "Kendra! I was afraid you might not come after all."

"I told you I would. Did you already sign your life away?"

"Yep."

"Well, let's get this over with." Taking Eve's arm, she started toward the common room's open doorway.

Eve glanced up, but the dark-haired girl was nowhere to be seen.

"What?" Kendra asked as they entered the main room. "What's bugging you now?"

"Nothing. I just got caught staring at a couple of sisters. It was stupid."

Kendra laughed. "You sure are jumpy, but then I guess you're supposed to be."

"Huh?"

"You're a cheerleader. You jump. It's natural." She smiled. "Come on, relax."

9

Malory Thomas stretched like a cat, her perfect body momentarily sated and looking exquisite against the rumpled red satin sheets on Professor Tongue's water bed. It was king-sized and clunky, a watery throwback that bounced and jounced and exuded warmth from beneath. Malory had owned one once herself, back when it was cool to have one.

Timothy Piccolo's water bed wasn't cool, but then neither was the good—the *very* good—professor. But both were kitschy, she decided, feeling kind. She glanced up, hearing the shower running, when the bathroom door opened. Steam curled about the man with the golden tongue as he peered out. "Care to join me in a hot shower?" he asked.

He was naked, a shortish sturdy man with moderate love handles and a dinky penis. It didn't matter much—the tongue was what made the man in this case. Some men couldn't reach a cervix with their dicks, the professor included; but he could hit it with that snake he hid in his mouth. And he was an artist. He could tap. He could rap. He could play Reveille.

He was so good at it that she thought it might be worth performing a little magic to keep him around, to keep him from aging further. Then again, men could become so boring so easily, even ones with special talents. Perhaps just a short extension . . .

"Well?" he asked.

"Start without me. I'll be in in a minute." No, she decided, when she was done here, she'd probably leave him behind when she moved on.

When he started singing in the shower, she smiled and knew it.

She rose from the bed and opened the window. Professor Tongue's little house was an old favorite of hers. A small craftsman-style cottage owned by the university, the century-old abode was only a brisk five-minute walk from Gamma House. Near the edge of the woods, its privacy was ensured by well-tended gardens, lots of trees and bushes. The university spent a fortune on gardeners; briefly she wondered if any of the administrators ever wondered why the place was so green, why the grass grew faster than theirs did at their homes. Probably not. The ones who lived in Greenbriar wouldn't realize it and the ones who commuted from Caledonia and farther places probably just thought it was the type of grass, or something in the soil. *And they'd be right.* . . .

Malory smiled at the chipmunk that chirped

at her from the branch of a young oak near the window. Whenever she spent time at Greenbriar, Malory ensconced her lovers in this cottage. When she discovered Professor Tongue's talents two years ago, she had promptly decided his off-campus excuse for an apartment wouldn't do; it was much too far away.

Fortunately, in no time at all, elderly Professor Higgins, a stuffy old English instructor who was then living here, one who had taught at the college for thirty years and looked at her oddly now and then, as if he might remember her from long ago, suffered a stroke that rendered him unable to speak a coherent sentence. He'd babbled like an idiot, but the university took pity on him and let him remain, so Malory had taken more drastic measures. More permanent ones. Higgins ceased his babbling for all time.

And Professor Tongue had been moved in before the old man was cold in the ground.

"Malory?"

Malory looked out at the tree and caught her breath as Brittany popped up from beneath the window, right in her face. She hid her annoyance. "Were you watching?"

Brittany nodded and produced a Peanut M&M from her pocket. "Yes." *Crunch, crunch.*

"Jealous?"

"You know it. Can I come in?"

"Are you forgetting something?"

Brittany looked cute and stupid. She was good at that. "What?"

"How's the pledge sign-up going?"

"Fine. Can I come in?"

Malory glanced at her watch. "It's five. I need to be there by six. I don't think it's a good idea."

Brittany dimpled up. "Please? Just for a few minutes."

"He's in the shower."

"So? Tell him to hurry up. I watched you guys for fifteen minutes. I *need* to come in."

Malory wanted to say no, but looking at that hopeful face, she just couldn't. Brittany was like a pet to her, but much more. She reached out and gently patted the girl's cheek. "Okay. Hurry up. I'll get Professor Tongue out of the shower. You get ready."

Leaving Brittany to climb in the window, Malory left to retrieve the professor. The good thing about tongues compared to cocks was that a good athletic one didn't need any downtime. She smiled. *Hmmm. Maybe I should keep him around.*

10

Professor Daniel S. McCobb, emeritus in age but not in practice, stood under an old-fashioned street lamp on the sidewalk across the campus road from Gamma House. He'd gone for a stroll after his last cultural anthropology class and the perfect weather had inspired him to walk farther than usual.

Once each year, usually in late September, as tonight, a marvelous harbinger occurred. On a night still warm with late summer, the first hint of autumn would appear. This was such a night. He loved it; the cool tang of fall riding the breeze, singing to him of fluttering golden leaves, the red glow of heat from a nearly finished fireplace log at midnight, of pumpkins on porches, Caledonia's Halloween parade, and hayrides along this very street at Greenbriar. In the old days, when the road was paved with cobblestones, the annual hayride was better. Asphalt just wasn't the same.

But the old sorority house, resting far back on its broad lawn across the way, hadn't

changed a bit. It was a monstrous piece of gen-
uine Greek Revivalist architecture. Six Ionic
columns ran across the front of the house, edging the wide wraparound veranda. The house
appeared to be two tall stories, but an attic was
hidden in the wide cornices below the roof and
behind the central pediment with its anthemia
ornamentation. Golden light shone from the
leaded entry-door sidelights and downstairs
windows. Above, about a third of the windows
were lit.

Something was going on at Gamma House
tonight; McCobb caught snatches of feminine
laughter on the autumn wind and saw figures
moving on the veranda. Since it was a week-
night, it probably wasn't initiations, but that
would be soon. *Bad stuff, that.* Initiation rituals
were rough in every culture. Meant to draw together individual personalities into a cohesive
whole, they served their purposes best in prim-
itive cultures where villages depended on each
member to ensure survival. Fraternity and
sorority initiations, in McCobb's opinion,
served little purpose. They ensured that young
people would learn loyalty born of fear and humiliation. They created young adults who knew
how to conform to the will of the majority, who
would do as they were told. Those who didn't
learn, who stayed but broke vows of secrecy,
were punished.

You old fool. This stuff's been toned town, especially

here at Greenbriar. Still, he felt a chill in his ancient bones, one having nothing to do with the slight hint of autumn. Fraternity hazings had stopped early in the seventies when a pledge drowned in the lake, and sororities were generally far gentler than the male societies.

Except for this one.

He had no proof, of course. But he'd been around a long time. He *knew* . . . He'd seen some things, researched others. He taught the only folklore classes on campus, and what would he be if he ignored the lore of Applehead Valley and Greenbriar University? *Not much, that's what.*

"Excuse me," said a woman's voice.

He stepped back as two girls approached from the path across the quad. "Pardon me, ladies."

The girls, a small blonde with all her curves on display and a taller, better-dressed girl with raven hair who exuded sexuality like perfume, passed him by; then the dark one paused and turned. The blonde pulled up short and turned as well, her eyes bright and cheeks flushed.

"Professor McCobb?" asked the dark one.

"Yes," he said, fascinated. A small trill of fear played up his spine, but at his age, it was easy to hide. "You know me," he said smoothly. "But I see so many students. I'm afraid you have the advantage, young lady."

Her dark eyes bored into him. He felt as if she could read his mind. "Malory Thomas," she said finally. "President of Gamma Eta Pi."

"Pleased to make your acquaintance," he said without offering his hand. "Are you in one of my classes?"

"No," she said. "I just know who you are. You're an author."

He smiled benignly. "Just some musty old papers."

"And a book of urban legends," Malory Thomas said. "I've read it."

He chuckled. "I'm still trying to live that down. I'm afraid that it amuses my colleagues to no end."

"It's cool," said the blonde. She wore so much lip gloss he was surprised it didn't drip.

"Thank you, Miss . . .?" *What are you calling yourself these days?*

"Brittany Woodcock. Gamma VP!"

"Miss Woodcock. I'm glad you enjoyed my little effort."

"I read it because of the title. The title was cool. *Is That a Hook in Your Pocket or Are You Just Glad to See Me?* That's just so cool." She popped something in her mouth and crunched it up. "So was the book."

"That was the publisher's title, I'm afraid. Granted, it sold better than my title would have—"

"Nice talking to you, Professor," Malory Thomas cut in. "I have to get to the house."

"We're showing the pledges around," Brittany called as she chased after Malory.

Watching them leave, Daniel McCobb allowed himself a small sigh of relief. He'd passed the test. The woman calling herself Malory Thomas didn't know he remembered her.

She hadn't aged a day.

Initiation

11

When Malory Thomas strutted into the drawing room, all the pledges stopped talking and stared at her. The sorority president silenced one stray giggle with the barest glance, and moved to stand in front of the huge fireplace. Brittany plopped her tight-jeaned butt down on a dusky rose floor pillow a few feet from her. She wore a green Gamma T-shirt with the Greek letters—ΓΗΠ—emblazoned in gold across her breasts. The letters were almost too stretched out to read and the shirt bottom had been tied in a knot below her bosom to show off her svelte waist and belly button ring.

Eve watched the little blonde stare adoringly at Malory and wondered if they were a couple. The girl seemed to stick to her like glue. Superglue. Meanwhile, Malory just stood there and gazed about the room, acting like royalty. She and the other officers wore the school and sorority colors in the form of long silky scarves with the Greek letters embroidered in gold thread prominently on the ends. They also wore enameled pins, delicate dark pink rosebuds on green stems. Each stem had two leaves and a few thorns, which seemed a little weird.

Watching Malory stand before the girls, Eve suspected she was basking in the pledges' terror and momentarily wondered why she wasn't feeling afraid herself, then decided the high-handed president pissed her off too much to scare her. *Who does she think she is?*

That's easy. She's the president of the most powerful sorority on campus. She has every right to act like an arrogant bitch. Eve quelled a burgeoning smile. Malory would never approve.

"Welcome to Gamma House," the president said, her voice as regal as her stance. "Over the next few weeks, you will attempt to earn your status as full sisters. During this time, and forevermore, you are sworn to keep all of our traditions and secrets safe from outsiders, and to take them with you to your grave. Are there any questions?" Her black eyes flashed over the pledges, daring them to speak.

Eve's skin crawled and she realized she was properly terrorized again. None of that had been on the paper she'd signed. The wording had been much gentler, more businesslike, like the nondisclosure paper she'd signed when she'd done volunteer work at the hospital the summer before last, where she just had to promise not to discuss any patients' conditions.

She glanced at Kendra, beside her on the sofa.

She was gazing down at her hands, her face serene, a hint of amusement curling up her lips. Eve realized her new friend wasn't intimidated at all and wondered why she didn't ask any questions. *For the same reason I'm not. She doesn't want to call that bitch's attention to herself.*

"Ladies," Malory said, "do you understand the gravity of the vows you are about to take? If you have any qualms, any notion that you might get drunk and tell a boyfriend or anyone else anything about the secrets of this sorority, I ask that you go to the desk, find your oath, and tear it in half, then leave. I am giving you this last chance to reconsider for your own good. To make this easier, we will take a five-minute break. I urge you all to get up and move around so that anyone who wishes to leave may do so without humiliation." Her smile was as cold as death. "Humiliating anyone is the last thing a Gamma sister wants to do."

12

Eve and Kendra glanced at each other and headed outside, coming to a halt on the veranda about twenty feet from the now-open entry doors. "What do you think?" Eve asked quietly.

Kendra shook her head. "I'm not sure what I think. It's probably the usual sorority nonsense, but you know that stuff I haven't told you about yet—the extra-secret stuff my granny told me about?"

Eve nodded. "What about it?"

"Not now and not here, Evie." She glanced around making sure no one had wandered close enough to hear her. "The thing is, it's probably all just hooey. Even Granny admitted that. But they could be serious about keeping secrets. You know about Skull and Bones?"

"Huh?"

"At Yale. It's a society that's super secret and really powerful. It grooms men for power positions. Both George and George Junior were members."

"The presidents? Of the United States?"

"Yes, those Georges. Other ones too, and all sorts of politicians and powerful types all over the world. It's really creepy."

"You're serious?" Eve asked. "I've heard of the Yale Lampoon—"

"Girl, that's the Harvard Lampoon and that's not what I'm talking about *at all*. That's funny stuff. Skull and Bones is *serious* stuff. And what might be going on here."

"But you're still going to pledge?" Eve asked in alarm.

"Sure. I don't think there're any secrets to worry about unless you get into that secret part."

"The Skull and Bones thing?"

"Yes, but don't say it anymore. If it's real, they're probably damned serious and you don't want to mess with that. You don't want them to know you even suspect unless they tell you about it."

"What if they tell?"

Kendra chuckled. "You're cute, you know that? They're not going to tell you anything, not now. Not until you're proven as a sister. But listen, the way that Heather fawned over you, you might be one of the ones they ask."

"What about you?"

Kendra shrugged. "I'm surprised they let me in at all. They check everybody out. You can be sure they know my granny's granny and the rest, right up the line, worked here."

"So they wouldn't want you because they worked here?"

Kendra opened her mouth, closed it, opened it again. "I don't mean because they *worked* here—because they were hired help. The one thing about Gamma that's good is that it isn't elitist." She laughed quietly. "I mean, it is, but only after you're in. The sorority itself is elite, but it chooses members from every income level and all kinds of backgrounds. Their thing is, they don't care what you were; they only care about what you become."

"Kind of like the army."

"Yeah. And that's a little scary too." She paused. "There's one girl here that's in my cultural iconography class."

"Your what?"

"It's one of Professor McCobb's classes. He's a folklore expert, among other things—the author of the urban legend book that's all over the student bookstore?"

"Sure. I know. So what about the girl?"

"Well, she's a really serious student. I don't really know her, I think she's six months or a year ahead of us—she's already a sister—but I think maybe she's snooping around."

"Why?"

"She's not the sorority type at all."

"And you are?" Eve grinned.

"Good point. Anyway, she's a journalism major, big time. And she's all over McCobb with questions. I think she's researching the sorority."

"Did you ask her?"

"Sort of. She just looked at me like I was nuts

and said that being a sorority member is good for future career opportunities. That's why she's in. And I didn't ask any more questions. That girl has a stare that's as intense as Malory's."

"Eww."

"It's not mean, though. Just intense—and I sure knew I wasn't supposed to ask any more questions. Don't let on I said anything."

"Of course not. Who is she?"

Kendra looked upward, thinking. "I'm blanking. I know her name—I hate brain farts. It's on the tip of my tongue—"

The pair looked at each other and snickered. "Bad word choice," Kendra said. "God, if I'm this bad at eighteen, what'll I be like at Granny's age? What's that girl's name?"

The porch lights flicked off and on twice, like a theater calling back its patrons. "I'll introduce you later, or poke you if she speaks up. Okay?"

Eve nodded. "So, are you up for this, Kendra?"

"The mysteries await." Kendra took her arm and they went back into the house.

13

The vows sounded serious and solemn. As Eve and the other pledges took them simultaneously, she actually thought they were pretty silly. Full of hooey, as Kendra would say. They had to stand in a half circle facing the fireplace and the officers while they repeated the words Malory spoke. The oath was dramatic as hell and used the phrase "to the death," several times, which really was goofy for a bunch of girls just out of high school to say. It felt as if they were playing a game of pretend, and probably that's exactly what they were doing.

It was intimidating nonetheless, especially since, just before the vows began, many more Gammas arrived, along with a couple of push-carts of folding chairs. Nice wooden ones with upholstered seats, not the usual gray metal things, Eve had noted approvingly. The sisters, perhaps two dozen of them, had set up their chairs at the far end of the room. Most wore jeans and green Gamma T-shirts, but a few wore the green silk scarves instead. Maybe pins too;

Eve couldn't tell in the brief instant she'd looked at the audience of sisters.

"Time for introductions," Veep Brittany chirped. She sounded like Alvin the Chipmunk's sister. "Heather, are all the sisters here?"

Heather, standing before the fireplace with Malory, Brittany, and the other officers, Teri and Michele, nodded. "I believe everyone is here?" She raised her voice and her eyes, looking toward the other end of the room.

A murmur arose among the Gammas, then someone said, "Everyone is present and accounted for, Madam Chairman."

Eve glanced at Kendra, who turned out to already be looking her way. Both let their eyes start to roll, but stopped short.

"Pledges, please take your seats," Malory ordered. She waited for them to settle in, then spoke again. "I'd like you each to stand and introduce yourself, tell us your long-range goals and why you want to be a Gamma." She nodded at the nearest pledge, the Chinese girl Eve had noticed the day before.

"I'm Nicole Chang, from Santa Cruz, California. I'm a biophysics major and I'd like to work in nanotechnology."

A brain. Anything having to do with numbers turned Eve off, and she'd bet her mother's batons that nanotechnology was something that involved math.

"I wish to be a Gamma sister in order to enjoy

the friendships that come with such a fine house, and of course to aid in my career, should I prove worthy. Thank you." The nervous girl sat down quickly.

And so it went. There were thirteen pledges and five more spoke as Eve nervously awaited her turn. Each one said basically the same thing about wanting to make friends and improve her career chances, but their majors varied greatly. There was a lit major, a drama, two biologies, and a linguistics.

And then Malory's eyes were on Eve. She rose. "I'm Eve Camlan, from Caledonia. I want to join the sorority to make friends and to help my career someday." She started to sit.

"Your career and your major are?" Malory said archly.

Eve felt herself blushing as she came back into full upright position. *My major is—What do I say? They all have majors picked out already!*

"Liberal arts," Kendra whispered.

"Liberal arts," Eve said. "For now. I'm not sure, but I think I'd like to be a teacher."

"Elementary?" Malory said, an eyebrow up, no smile anywhere.

"No. Junior high or high school." *Let me die now.*

"Malory, everyone," said Heather, "Eve Camlan is an award-winning cheerleader and I sincerely hope she wants to try out for our squad. I think she'll outshine all of us."

Bless you. "Thanks. I'd like to try," she managed, then sank into her seat.

Kendra did much better. She didn't mention her interest in folklore, but said she wanted to be a cultural anthropologist. Eve smiled at her as she sat down.

Two more girls introduced themselves. One was in premed, the other an English major. And then came the girl with the fiery hair and intense green eyes.

"I'm Merilynn Morris."

Eve's stomach dropped. She had hoped the girl wouldn't come back. The lake, the storm, the eyes came rushing back.

"I'm from Santo Verde, California, and I haven't decided on my major yet."

"Any clues, dear?" Malory asked.

"Not yet," Merilynn said, obviously not intimidated. "I'm a dabbler."

"You must have some long-term goals. I'm sure you listed something on your application."

The girl paused, then said serenely, "Chemistry. I might become a chemist."

"The kind that cures cancer or makes perfume?" the president inquired.

"Maybe I'll make perfume that cures cancer," Merilynn replied. "I wanted to join Gamma because I'm told my mother was a sister."

"You were *told?*" Malory actually smiled. It was hideous.

"She died shortly after I was born, so yes, I was told."

"I don't remember seeing any mention of this on your application."

"Well, Malory, I wanted to get in on my own, not as a legacy."

The president nodded, evidently satisfied by the answer. Merilynn sat down and Eve relaxed slightly.

The final two pledges—a poly sci and another English major—spoke; then Malory asked the sisters in the audience to introduce themselves. Eve listened, but not as well as she might have. Exhaustion was overtaking her. Then Kendra poked her as one of the sisters rose. It was the one with shortish dark hair that she'd seen on the landing earlier.

"My name is Samantha Penrose. I'm going to be a journalist."

Eve felt dizzy as more memories swept over her. She'd never expected to see either of these girls again. She hadn't seen them in years and years. She didn't want to see them. And here they were. Both of them.

"Hey, are you all right?" Kendra whispered, touching her hand.

Eve nodded.

"What's wrong?" Kendra mouthed.

Eve bent slightly and whispered in her ear, "Déjà vu."

14

"You want to meet her?" Kendra asked as they began a half hour of mingling, new sisters and old, after the ceremony.

"Who?"

"The girl I told you about from my cultural iconography class. Sam Penrose. I poked you when she spoke. You felt that, right?"

"Yes." Eve was having trouble concentrating. Knowing that both her old acquaintances from cheer camp, the two that had shared the nightmarish adventures, were in the same room with her now, was upsetting, even though she knew it shouldn't be, even though she had known it would probably happen. *You should say hello, long time no see, and be done with it. They probably don't want to hash over old times any more than you do.*

"Evie, come on," Kendra said, hauling her to a corner in the rear where a crystal punch bowl sat on a long narrow tapestry runner on an antique sideboard. Plates of munchies—cookies, chips, dip, veggies—surrounded it. She ladled punch into a crystal cup and handed it to Eve, then made one for herself. "What's up with you?" she asked.

Eve studied the punch cup. "This looks like real crystal. But that would be nuts."

"Speaking of nuts, check it out." Kendra nodded toward another small table where Brittany was scooping up peanuts from a bowl and putting them in her pockets. It was hard work; those skintight pockets didn't hold much. The veep glanced up, saw them looking at her, and a black look flashed through her eyes. Eve could almost feel the anger in it—but it was gone quickly, replaced with a smile, wide and cheerful. She took more nuts and popped them in her mouth and wandered off without a word. Not that she could say anything with so many nuts in her mouth. "How does she keep her figure?" Kendra said with a chuckle.

"I don't know. She must have the metabolism of a hummingbird. She's always eating." Eve sipped her drink thirstily.

Kendra grinned. "Your punch pleases you?"

"It does." Eve refilled her cup and snagged a carrot stick.

"Okay, so are you going to tell me what's scaring you?"

"Nothing."

"Come on. You're one of those social butterflies. Don't try and deny it—I know your type."

"I'm not—"

"Come on, I'm teasing you. Where's your

sense of humor? You're a cheerleader but your perkiness is missing. What's bugging you?"

"It's stupid."

"Tell me anyway."

"Samantha Penrose?"

"What about her?"

"She was the other girl on Applehead Island with me—she and Merilynn Morris were both there."

"Really? Sam's the brainiac you talked about?" Eve nodded.

"I believe you. So what's the problem?"

"I don't know. I just don't want to talk to her. Or Merilynn. I don't want them to be here. I wish they weren't."

"Did you guys fight or something?"

"No. I just don't want to have to talk about old times."

Kendra studied her a long moment. "That was some scary stuff."

"It was."

15

"Excuse me!"

As Heather Horner approached, the central point in a V of seven girls, Kendra smiled, amused by their Barbie-ness; even though they came in several colors, they were all cast from the same mold. *Cheerleaders.* She glanced at Eve; she was beaming. *She recognizes her own kind.* Kendra smiled. Eve had the same look, but maybe because she'd gotten to know her, she could see more than the Barbie-doll mask. She could see vulnerability and sensitivity behind the bright smile and she hoped that it wouldn't disappear under the influences of this gaggle of giggling airheads. *You don't know they're airheads. Don't be such a snob. At least for Evie's sake.*

"Hi, Eve, hi, Kendra," Heather said. Kendra saw her glance at her name tag, but not at Eve's. *She's a cheerleader. She's mentally incapable of remembering everyone's name.*

"What?" Heather asked, seeing Kendra's smile.

"Nothing. Just happy to be here."

Heather nodded. "I wanted to introduce you

to my squad. You've met our secretary and treasurer, Teri and Michele, already, right?"

The two shook hands with Eve, then Kendra.
"Are you a cheerleader?" Michele asked, obviously being polite.

"No, just an onlooker."

"Meet the rest of the squad," Heather said, gesturing. "This is Julie, this is Jeannie, this is Jenny,
and last but not least, this is Ginny."

What, no Joanie? The cookie-cutout girls, giggling greetings, were all over Eve, hugging her
like old friends, barely sparing nods for Kendra.
*Maybe this is the secret society. A secret society of cheer-
leaders. Now* there's *a scary thought!*

"So, guess what, Eve!" Heather bubbled.

"What?"

"Normally, anyone chosen this weekend for
tryouts would be a substitute only until next year,
but this time, whoever's the very best of the newbies will get to join the squad immediately. It'll
be lots of hard work." Heather winked. "But we
need a replacement right away."

"One of you is leaving?"

"She already left." The squad cast their eyes
down as one. "She died. It was terrible."

"That's awful! I'm so sorry. May I ask . . . what
happened? Have I met her?"

"I don't think you met her," Heather said. "I
think she went missing the night of the rush.
We thought maybe she'd just run off for a
while—we *prayed* she had—but they found

Mulva's body just a few hours ago." She glanced around furtively. "We didn't want to bring it up and spoil the evening."

"Will there be services?"

"Just a little memorial among ourselves. Frankly, nobody liked her very much."

"That's pretty cold," Kendra said.

Heather shot her a harsh glance. "You didn't know her. I won't speak ill of the dead, but she had us all fooled. She wasn't what she appeared to be."

"What happened?" Kendra couldn't stop herself. "Did she tell some sorority secrets?"

Heather was a statue for a second; then she re-animated, all warmth and understanding. "Of course not. You don't think—" She paused dramatically, then put her arm around Kendra, giving her a quick squeeze. "Sweetie, that stuff is just talk, you know that. And I guess that did sound cold. It's just that, well, Mulva had problems."

"What kind of problems?" Eve asked.

"Heroin, for one thing. Can you imagine a Gamma Eta Pi with a *drug* problem? Especially a cheerleader? It's against everything we stand for. And she knew she could come to her sisters to help solve the problem, but she didn't. Instead, she even tried to talk Jenny into getting high with her."

"She did," one of the J-clones said solemnly.

"That's still cold," Kendra said. "Maybe she was embarrassed."

"When Jenny wouldn't take heroin with her, she tried to give it to her while she was asleep."

"What?" Kendra asked. "How?"

"She put some in her mouth."

"She tried to put it under my tongue," the clone said, "but I woke up."

"What happened?"

"I got really sick."

"But that's not all," Heather said.

"What else?" Kendra asked.

Instead of replying, Heather nodded at the other girls. "Tell her."

"She tried to give it to me," said one.

"And me," said another.

"And me," the third said, her eyes like saucers.

"She was trying to turn *my* squad into *drug addicts*. Can you imagine?"

"That's pretty bad," Kendra said. *And it sounds like bullshit.*

"Once, she even approached Teri and Michele, *officers* of the *sorority!* Can you *imagine?*"

"It's pretty hard to imagine."

"And that's not all," Heather said yet again.

"What else?" Kendra asked, thinking they were being fed a whole silo of shit.

"She peed in Malory's lemonade."

Eve giggled nervously.

"How do you know that?" Kendra asked.

"Malory caught her. Malory loves lemonade. Our housekeeper, Mildred, makes a special batch just for her. It's in a different container."

"That's weird," Kendra said.

"No. Malory likes it without any sweetener."

"Oh." *Why doesn't that surprise me?*

"And—"

"That's not all," Kendra finished, crossing her arms. "So, what are the other reasons that you aren't mourning her death?"

"Ex-Lax in the hot chocolate."

"Old trick. Not a biggie."

"On Parent Night?"

"Okay, that's pretty nasty."

"You're not kidding," said either Michele or Teri, the officer-clones. "Housekeeper wouldn't clean the toilets."

"You didn't make Mulva clean them?" Kendra asked.

"She took off. We couldn't leave them dirty until she came back," Heather explained.

"They were really, really dirty," said one of the J-clones.

"She used *a lot* of Ex-Lax!" added another.

"It was like really stinky modern art," said one more.

"Stinky," added the forth J-clone, sounding a little like Homer Simpson thinking about chili burgers.

"Why did you accept her as a member if she was like this?"

"Like I said, she fooled everyone. We had no idea. She was a champion cheerleader back at her high school in French Lick."

"In what?"

"French Lick," Heather said, all seriousness. "It's in Indiana."

A J-clone started to giggle. Heather shot her a look worthy of Malory. The giggle stopped. "You can look it up."

"I've heard of it," Kendra said.

"She was a farm girl," Teri or Michele said. "She must have been on the edge and we think that moving to a place like this probably put her over the top."

"A place like this?"

"You know, with mountains and the ocean. She was used to the plains."

"Flatland," said the other Michele or Teri.

"Not used to the big city," Kendra said. She added a slight smile, deciding at the last instant not to bait them further. She'd play along.

Heather smiled back. "That's funny."

"Maybe it's true," Eve said. "If she ever went to a big place like San Francisco, maybe it freaked her out."

Eve obviously thought that Indiana was something out of a corn-fed musical. No cities. Maybe no airports. Kendra had a sudden desire to drag Eve kicking and screaming out of the sorority house before she turned into one of *them*. *The Stepford Cheerleaders.*

Maybe you should just drag yourself out of here. Maybe you're the one who doesn't belong here.

"Attention, attention!" Malory stood in the entryway and clapped her hands sharply. "Quiet, please." She only had to wait a few seconds before silence reigned.

"We're going to take you pledges on house tours now. Heather, Michele, and Brittany will escort you." She beckoned at the girls and they went to join her, leaving Kendra and Eve alone among the J-clones.

"Please divide yourselves up into groups."

"Come on," Eve said to Kendra and headed straight for Heather. Kendra followed.

16

"Okay," Heather told Eve, Kendra, and two other pledges. "Stay with me. No dawdling or wandering off on your own."

With that, she led them through the first floor. "Everyone stay together," Heather Horner repeated. "No wandering off on your own. First of all, the room you've spent all your time in so far, we call the drawing room."

"Why?" asked a short pledge. She had golden brown hair and glasses and according to her name tag, she answered to "Lou."

Heather smiled. "Why not? That's what it's always been called. Now come along." She led them into the hall and turned right, showing them the parlor, which was a room like the drawing room but about half the size. The furniture was older and less pristine. Chairs and two couches were arranged informally around coffee and side tables near the smaller fireplace. Several of the sisters were already curled up on the furniture. Their books and notepads scattered across the nearest

120 *Tamara Thorne*

low table. "Let's let them study," said their guide, then led them on.

"When it was built, the house had all the modern conveniences," Heather told them. "The wall sconces used to be gas lamps. Today, of course, they've been wired for electricity. Until a few years ago, all of the power lines were in pipes running along the outside of the walls." She smiled as she led them down a connecting hall with tall double-hung windows sheathed in sheer eggshell curtain panels. Paintings of Greenbriar and environs punctuated the wall space between the windows. One painting of Applehead Lake gave Eve a shiver. It was dark with a storm-clouded sky and black water, the island with its skeletal trees a dark silhouette.

"Gamma House was very quaint," Heather continued. "Fortunately, our alumni have helped fund continuing renovations and modernizations. It's very expensive keeping up a house like this. Far more expensive than tearing it down and rebuilding, but it's worth it. The house has such history. Here's the kitchen."

She took them down a short flight of steps and into a cavernous room. "What do you think?"

"It's amazing," Kendra said. The others ah'd their agreements.

"The refrigerators and dishwashers are modern, of course. The stoves date from the thirties."

"The microwave doesn't look too new either," Kendra said.

Heather laughed. "It's at least ten years old.

We keep it because it still works and it's huge. There are three new ones over there, on the long counter under the glass-fronted cabinets."

Eve took her eyes off the three old stoves and looked at the long counter, cabinets above and below. The glass inserts in the upper doors were thick and wavy-looking, sort of art deco, she thought. The lower cabinets' contents were hidden behind simple painted wooden doors.

"The kitchen was redone in the thirties, new cabinets and everything," Heather verified. "Of course, it's pretty quaint now too. We may work on a fund to remodel it—new cabinets and all."

"I love it as it is," Eve said.

"Me too." Kendra looked around. "Before it was redone, most of the cabinets were open. The top ones. Everything was painted white."

"You've been reading up on the house?" Heather asked.

"No. Several generations of my family worked here."

She said it nonchalantly, but Eve could see defiance in her eyes as she waited for rude remarks, or maybe just rude looks. None appeared.

"You must know some stories about the old days," Heather said. "Maybe you can tell some sometime."

"I doubt I know any stories you don't," Kendra replied, gazing steadily at the other girl.

"Oh? Okay. You guys want to see the dumbwaiter?"

17

Kendra knew there was a passage from a door in the corner of the kitchen that led deeper into the ground into a root cellar, and another that led across the rear yard to an old smokehouse, but Heather had mentioned neither one. The tunnel would be all blocked off, probably damaged by earthquakes over the years. The smokehouse's roof could be seen among the trees, but it wasn't in use even when Granny worked there, so Kendra guessed it was locked up tight now. It was one of the places the ghost of Holly Gayle was supposed to appear. Kendra said nothing, but quietly let herself be led into the cellar where a monstrous old boiler sat in summer dormancy. It would come into use again soon, Heather said, explaining that the heating had yet to be upgraded. Another fund-raising project down the road. They hoped to get rid of the window air conditioners scattered throughout the house as well, but it would require plenty of effort and Gamma spirit. Kendra managed not to roll her eyes over that phrase. *What am I doing here?*

They climbed the stairs to the second floor, Kendra admiring the banister and rails gleaming darkly, the patina of age polished to a high shine. "No wonder your housekeeper wouldn't clean the bathrooms. She must spend all her time waxing the woodwork."

"Mildred has enough to do without polishing everything. I'm afraid that's the job of our new sisters," Heather said, showing dimples. "That means you guys take it over as soon as you move in."

"For how long?" Kendra was fuming, feeling used, but could see the other girls were barely dismayed at the idea.

"Until next year. We all have jobs helping around the house, but as newbies, you get the worst. You also divvy up the noncarpeted floors with the sophomores."

"What do the other girls do?" asked Neelie, the other pledge, a willowy studious type, the poly sci major.

"Sophomores do windows and floors. Juniors vacuum. Seniors supervise."

"I guess so," Kendra muttered.

"What?"

"So, I guess all the bedrooms are on this floor?" She smiled, something warning her not to piss off Heather.

"Yes, they are, except for the two guest and/or broken-leg bedrooms downstairs. I forgot to show you those. You can see them later. Okay, this is important. Listen up: never, ever go into the east wing on this floor. It's off-limits. Totally, absolutely off-limits."

"Why?" Lou asked.

"Is it unsafe?" Neelie chimed in.

"A lot of it is uninhabited at this point—the rooms need to be restored. The rest makes up the senior section." She looked at Eve. "And some cheerleaders also get to room there. We have separate rooms there and only two girls to a bathroom. But that's all you need to know about that. You'll be sharing rooms in the west wing. Come on. There are thirteen of you and five available rooms. Three rooms have three beds each and the other two are doubles. Your roommates are your choice, of course."

Kendra glanced at Eve, wondering if she really wanted to room with a cheerleader. Eve saw her look, misread it, and squeezed her hand. "Roomie?" she asked silently. Kendra nodded. It was fate.

18

"I *love* this room!" Eve cried as she dragged Kendra back to a two-bed room after the tour. "Do you love it?"

Kendra looked around. It was beautiful if you liked pastels. The ceilings—normal height on this floor—were white with decorative molding. The walls were painted a light delicate color that Kendra wanted to believe was peach. They were nearly peach. Pinkish peach. She didn't like the idea of a pink room.

"Don't you love the color scheme?"

"Not really my colors, Eve, but it will do."

"You don't like it?" Eve asked, stricken. "We can take that other room, the blue one."

"No, this is fine. I really didn't like that blue one anyway. It seemed cold."

"I love the bedspreads. Do you?"

Kendra looked at the dainty floral pattern and tried not to wince. "I can live with them. What I like is this window." She reached across the small desk beneath it and drew the curtain back—*too frilly*—and looked out at the fifty feet of back lawn, the gardens, a tiny pond, and the old smokehouse, at the edge of the forest. From here, she could see more of it—the top half. The windows were shuttered. Undoubtedly, the door was locked. It fascinated her, maybe because of Granny's stories. She wanted to see inside. "Eve, look." She pointed out the smokehouse.

Eve joined her at the window. "The forest is spooky. I didn't think about that. Do you like looking at it?"

"Sure. And the smokehouse. That's what I wanted to show you."

Eve looked some more. "I don't think I like it either. It's forbidding." She paused. "Do you want the bed by the window? The desk under the window?"

"You bet. You're okay with that?"

"Am I ever!" Eve left the window and went to the other side of the room, plopping down on the windowless bed, by the windowless desk. "You're sure?'

"Absolutely. I love the view."

19

Eve sailed through the cheerleading tryouts.
She was good at all the positions, topper, bottom,
and her kicks and splits went perfectly. She tried
out with cheers based on ones she'd made up for
other tryouts, gearing them now to the Greenbriar Knights football team. At first nervous, she
soon forgot her fears in the excitement of the
moment; cheering took her to another place, a
place where she never lacked confidence, a place
where she felt at her best and most alive. Eight
other girls, four of them Gammas, including little Lou from last night's tour, tried out as well,
and only the Gamma members made the cut,
even though a couple of the other girls, in Eve's
opinion, were more talented. One Gamma member didn't make it either.

"You'll serve as substitutes for the rest of the
year," Heather told the four after the others left
the gym. "All but one of you, that is. The girl with
the top score becomes part of the squad immediately and will have to practice really hard
because she'll be cheering in tomorrow night's

game against the Fort Charles Dragons. Who feels up to that?"

Eve shot her hand up without thinking twice, and she would have even if she hadn't already known she was the chosen one. The others put their hands up haltingly. What Heather was asking—learning routines in a day—was nearly impossible. *Unless you're almost a pro,* Eve thought proudly.

"Eve, I'm glad you're eager to do it because you outscored everyone today. You're the new full member of the squad. Congratulations!"

"Thank you! Thank you so much!" Eve bubbled, happily enduring a round of hugs and congratulations.

"Thank you, Eve! We're proud to have you," Heather said at last. "The rest of you will practice, too. As subs, you have to know the routines. You will all be called upon to fill in this year. Are you ready?"

The girls agreed happily.

"You never know," Heather said. "We may need a sub tomorrow night, so I want you all to practice like mad."

"What about uniforms?" Eve asked.

"Don't worry, we have them ready for you all. Now, you girls go into the locker room and do whatever you need to do to get ready to work your asses off. We," she said, gesturing at the six cheerleaders behind her, "will work with you individually and together for a couple of hours.

We'll have a dinner break, and then more practice. Okay. Any questions?"

Lou raised her hand.

"Yes?"

"I was just wondering . . . Did you begin the year without any substitutes?"

"Good question. Yes, we did. Jenny and Ginny were our newest graduates from subbing. We had two more, but they didn't come back after summer vacation. We had intended to bring them on and expand the squad size by two, but it didn't work out. And then, as you may know, we lost Mulva Delacourt, an experienced cheerleader, which is why we have to bring one of you right onto the squad."

"Excuse me," Eve said.

"Yes?"

"I just wondered what happened to her? You said someone found her body? Does that mean she was murdered? If it's okay to ask."

Heather studied her so long that Eve's stomach was in knots by the time the other girl replied. "We don't know what happened to her. We probably never will, not for sure, but she probably went off into the woods, overdosed, and got lost. I'm afraid that there wasn't much left—just some bones. Animals got to the body. There's not much to autopsy." She shook her head regretfully. "We don't know for sure, but it will probably be ruled death by misadventure." She paused. "We do ask that none of you talk about the incident to outsiders."

"What does that mean exactly?" Eve asked.

"It means you don't answer any questions or ask any. It's terrible that it happened, but we can't let it ruin our school spirit. As cheerleaders, ladies, it's out job to keep morale tip-top. Got it?"

"Got it," Eve murmured.

"Could she have been murdered?" Lou asked. "I heard there was a serial killer in the woods."

"That serial killer story has been around for a century, so the killer would have to be pretty old by now." Heather smiled. "I wouldn't worry about that. But, girls, it's not a good idea to wander around the forest. Things do happen. In the woods."

"Then she could be a murder victim," Lou persisted.

"No. She was just another victim of drug abuse. Now, go get ready for a real practice!"

With that, the new girls cheered and dashed off to the lockers, Eve in the lead. She pushed the dead girl from her mind, deciding to ask Kendra about legends of killers and rapists later.

20

"Brittany," Malory said, rubbing her gently behind one ear.

The blonde looked up into Malory's dark eyes. "Huh?"

"What do you think of Eve Camlan?"

Brittany nestled her head comfortably in Mal's lap. "I think she'll be perfect. You made an excellent choice. Don't stop."

Malory renewed her petting, now moving her hand to Brittany's forehead, smoothing away the hair. If the girl had been a cat, she'd purr. Instead, she reached, eyes closed, for a handful of sunflower seeds from a package resting against her side.

"Do you think she's full of juice, Brittany?"

"Very full. She's ripe and ready. She'll be perfect." The girl opened her eyes and gazed into her mistress's. "Feed me?"

"You're spoiled," Malory said, but she took the seeds from Brittany's palm and started feeding her one at a time. "I don't know why I do this for you. You don't deserve it."

"Sure I deserve it. I always deserve it. What would you do without me?"

"I have no idea, you little brat. I have no idea."

They stayed as they were for a long time, Malory sitting on the overstuffed green velvet sofa in her room, Brittany sprawled across it, Malory's lap her pillow. They drew energy from one another and in doing so, strengthened their individual and combined power.

Malory could live without her; at one time, many, many years ago, she had. But when she cast out a call for a familiar, a companion, here in this very wood, long before it was called Applehead, Brittany had answered. It happened one warm summer night. After performing her sorcery, Malory had gone to sleep near the spot where the deserted chapel now stood, barely a mile from here, hidden among the oak and pine in a very old place of power. When she awoke, Brittany was there beside her, watching her with those bright, inquisitive eyes. She had been alone longer than Malory, waiting long years for the right mistress to call her. They were meant to be together.

And that, Malory knew, was why she put up with the girl's constant demands and need for attention. Sometimes she wanted to boot her across the room—and had, occasionally, when she truly deserved it—but they always made up. They were two powerful beings entwined to make one far more powerful one. And they loved each other loyally, always sharing everything, from plates of food to lovers. Often, Brittany left her adjoining bedroom and slept with Malory. There was sex, but not often unless a man joined them; their desire to be together was born of their need for one another. Their love was pure.

And that was just about the only pure thing about either of them.

Malory smiled sleepily as Brittany nibbled the last sunflower seed from her fingers, then pulled the hand down between her breasts. She loved to have her belly rubbed.

"Mmmm, harder."

Malory scratched Brittany's side gently with her fingernails. One of the girl's legs wiggled a little in time with the scratching. "Brittany?"

"Hmmm?"

"What do you think of Professor Tongue?"

"I think he's an arrogant nerd, but I don't care because of what he can do."

"Do you mind his small penis?"

"Why?" Her eyes opened. "Could you put a spell on it, make it bigger?"

"We've tried that before, my sweet. It doesn't work too well, remember? It's too hard to control the size."

"Remember that man who lived in Applehead Valley? That big blond farmer?" Brittany laughed sleepily.

"That's exactly who I was thinking of." Jake Vanderdickens had been a handsome, strapping man, tall with broad shoulders and a full beard of gold spun with red. He reminded Malory of her brother, dead so many years, but that didn't diminish her ardor; after all, she had seduced him as well. The poor idiot had nearly killed himself when he found out he had fucked his sister while under a glamour that made him mistake her for his wife. Malory chuckled. Jake excited her partly because of that forbidden night of lust with her own brother. And she excited Jake, who often left his family on moonlit nights to meet her in the forest and make love on a fragrant bed of pine needles and ferns, on the place of power.

Jake was a skilled lover, or was once Malory had taught him the art. He, like Timothy Piccolo, had a long tongue and used it masterfully. It wasn't as long or as talented as the professor's, but it was a fine instrument nonetheless. Unfortunately, like Piccolo, he had a bantam-sized cock. And one day Malory, with Brittany's help, tried to change its dimensions.

The next night, when he came to her, what hung between his legs was a monster; the width of his strong arm, it hung almost to his knees at rest and resembled a baseball bat once aroused. At the same time, his tongue nearly disappeared, shrinking to a nubbin of its former size. Malory knew she had broken some law of nature, something to do with balance and power. She'd sent him home unsatisfied and that night, while she was trying to figure out how to fix what she had damaged, Jake accidentally fucked his wife, Moira, to death. Moira was the daughter of the Applehead Valley police chief and the next morning, when he came by and found Jake crying by the body, he arrested him. Filled with grief and fury, the chief paid some roughs to spirit Jake from his jail cell the next night and see that the man, whose only crime was being too well hung, was well hung by the neck, from the limb of an old oak.

Intrigued, Malory had since tried variations on the spell on men who didn't really matter to her, men who matched the criteria of long tongue and small genitalia. It was always the same. She'd also tried it on women, casting spells to increase breast size, but it always resulted in shrinkage that made their asses look like old men with stoved-in cheeks. It was, she thought, something to do with distribution of mass. You couldn't really change the physicality of a mere human, one lacking any magical capability, without consequences. Humans were no different from other animals; they were made of simple stuff. She smiled, thinking about her long-ago mentor's story about how he'd accidentally created the platypus. "Sometime," she told Brittany softly, "it might be fun to find a man with a huge nose, a normal tongue, and a small cock. That might work better."

"Give him a nose job?" She giggled merrily.

"Um-hmm. And a dick enlargement."

"Noses are different from tongues and cocks though," her familiar cautioned, giving Malory a glimpse of the old wisdom she usually kept hidden. "Those are similar in texture. Noses are full of cartilage. You might get something monstrous."

"Like a cock that never softened?"

Brittany smiled. "If you're lucky." She stretched and turned on her side, burrowing her nose into Malory's navel, her warm breath tickling her abdomen. "So why were you thinking about Professor Tongue?"

Malory understood the muffled words only because of long practice. "I was thinking of giving him an extension. Keeping him at the age he is now."

"For how long?"

"I don't know. We have to switch locations next year. If I magicked him, we could take him with us. If we want to leave him behind, well, it would be a pity to come back here in twenty years and have him be old and decrepit. What do you think? Should I do it?"

"How much would it cost?"

"For two decades without any aging? The life of a mindless loser ought to do the trick. I wouldn't need much power."

"It doesn't have to be a virgin or anything?"

"Not at all. It can be a chicken fucker with an IQ of twenty-three."

"Well, then, Malory, I think you should think

about it. There's plenty of time to decide." She turned her face up to her mistress, a slow wicked smile on her lips. "I think you should spend that time testing his stamina and skill and that you should let me help you."

Malory bent and brushed her lips lightly against Brittany's. "Of course. Don't I always?"

21

Standing on the Greenbriar football field, waiting for a cue from Heather to begin another cheer, Eve knew that if she hadn't been so excited about cheering for the first time, she would have dropped from exhaustion. Heather and the other girls had pushed all the newbies to the limit and beyond and Eve received the biggest push of all. It had been like a cheerleader boot camp, drilling and drilling and then drilling some more. She was glad she'd kept up with her aerobics and dancercise; it had kept her from collapsing.

Today, she awoke with stiff burning muscles and spent twenty minutes in the dorm showers easing the soreness away with hot water. By the time she hit her morning classes she felt good despite her muscular exhaustion. At noon, she'd gone to join the other girls for more practice, feeling only a little wicked at skipping out on her afternoon classes. The practice went on until four o'clock and by then, Eve felt pretty confident. The new subs fared decently except for little Lou, who had to sit out the last hour. Eve felt sorry for her, knowing the girl felt humiliated and weak even though she'd withstood far more than any average coed could.

After practice, they showered and had a picnic at a table in a little patio area outside the gym brought to them by Mildred McArthur, the housekeeper and cook, who didn't polish wood or clean windows or bathrooms. The woman was a glaring troll, tall and broad with a Neanderthal brow and dark steel-gray hair, the color of clouds ready to burst. She reminded Eve of Mrs. Van Dyke, a nightmarish PE teacher in tenth grade.

She wore a very dated dress the same stern color as her tightly bunned hair. Almost military, the shirtwaisted statement of nonfashion had long sleeves neatly folded up to just below her elbows, shoulder pads, and a breast pocket holding a small notebook and pen. Mildred had buttoned it over her massive bosom, all the way up to her chin. Blackish hose and black leather clunker shoes—the sensible old-fashioned kind that couldn't be as comfortable as modern ones—completed the outfit.

Eve shrunk back as the woman approached, bearing a massive wicker picnic basket. Heather introduced the subs to her and she stared each one down in turn, never saying a word or even nodding. She just set the basket on the table and stalked off.

"You'll get used to her," Heather said as a couple of the J-clones opened the basket and began setting out paper plates, cups, utensils, and finally an array of food fit for a king's feast. Heather opened a purple jug and poured equally purple liquid from it into the cups. "This is Mildred's special energy drink. We don't quite know what she puts in it, but it's good once you're used to it, and it'll bring you all back to life. Everybody drink up before you eat. We have Gatorade and bottles of water to have with your food."

Eve thought it was grape juice until she put the cup to her lips. It was more like blackberries, raspberries, and blueberries, all mixed up together, very tasty except for a peculiar herby undertaste. She drank quickly, her eyes on the food containers.

Roast chicken pieces, strips of turkey breast, and bloody-looking paper-thin slices of rare roast beef were revealed. A little pot of horseradish wafted deliciously, making Eve zero in on the beef that went with it even though she usually skipped red meat. There were thin slices of cucumber and red onion, flowered radishes, perfect lettuce leaves. Tomatoes, shredded bell peppers in three colors, and pots of fresh salsa completed the vegetable menu. Carbs were less abundant—there was pita bread, very thin pumpernickel slices, and a container of hot steaming flour tortillas. Fresh pineapple, kiwi, papaya, and mango chunks served as dessert.

And as Eve ate, she understood why they put

up with the dour Mildred McArthur. The woman was a wizard with food.

When they were done, they talked and planned, then finally went to dress for the game. Eve's green and gold uniform fit perfectly, which wasn't too surprising since there was a lot of Spandex involved. The bottom—a short skirt with attached panties—was simple, the hem and navel-revealing waistline edged in gold. The cropped midriff top was sleeveless and had the Knight's insignia, a golden shield, emblazoned on it.

"You look great, Eve," Heather said, catching her admiring herself in the mirror.

Eve blushed. She'd never worn a uniform so sexy and revealing. "So do you."

Behind Heather, the rest of the squad gathered and Eve saw that each of the regulars had a red rosebud tattooed on her hip. The green stems disappeared under the uniform bottom.

"Uh, the roses—" Eve began.

Heather smiled. "Cute, aren't they? She linked her arm in Eve's. "We'll talk later. Right now we have football players to cheer to a big win! Let's go, girls!"

22

Professor Daniel McCobb had stayed late grading papers, and leaving for Caledonia just before the game began, had to wait for streams and trickles of students crossing the campus road as they made their way to the bright lights of the stadium. Everything had looked right and he felt a little of the old thrill. He hadn't gone to a game in years but at that moment, with the scent of fall spurring his sense of nostalgia, he was briefly tempted to look in.

And he might have done it, but Vera had phoned to tell him their son, Dennis, had arrived for the weekend and that they and her pot roast with mashed potatoes, gravy, and baby glazed carrots were waiting for his arrival. *And baked apples. Don't forget those!*

His stomach growled an order to hurry home. He complied. Exiting the campus grounds, he turned left onto Greenbriar Road, then took a quick right on the old road that bypassed the tiny town itself. Applehead Road ran just inside the edge of the forest, passing only trees and a few crumbling stone buildings left over from Greenbriar's brief halcyon years. It curved along the hillside past the road leading into the cheer-leading camp on the lake, and then another mile where it again joined with Greenbriar Road and the cutoff for the Pacific Coast Highway and Caledonia. Applehead Road ran him a mile out of the way, but it was generally much faster than braving the town's overly civilized route. One could only stand so many stop signs in one's life-time.

Even though it was not yet fully dark, McCobb turned on his high beams as soon as the last campus light was hidden behind the trees. Applehead Road was gloomy on all but the sunniest days, the tall thick pines looming over the road, the oaks, still green, filling in spaces where the sun might dare to cast a ray.

A deer ran onto the road and paused, caught in the headlights. McCobb, unsurprised, tapped the brakes to slow and honked the deer back into action. Its white tail disappeared into the trees as he passed.

He slowed again as the road became a squiggle. His headlights flashed over the ruins of an old Wells Fargo office from the days of the Pony Express, half-walls of stone, a few old timbers on the ground. The mild switchback then caused illumination of the other side of the road, the deep forest side. Somewhere beyond those trees lay the old Greenbriar Chapel, a place rumored to be the

home of various unholy (at least to Christians) beings, the primary one being the Greenbriar Ghost
or "green ghost" as it was usually called. At one
time, it was also referred to as the "forest knight,"
but few knew that name anymore.

McCobb realized he'd slowed to a bare crawl as
he peered into the forest. He thought he saw a
flickering light moving among the trees. *Idiot students.* The young never learned. They loved to go
to the chapel ruins to drink and grope one another; it didn't matter that another dead coed
had been found out here, that many bodies—too
many for coincidence—had littered the woods
over the years. No, the excitement of the stories
of the Greenbriar Ghost—which wasn't even a
ghost but really a nature elemental according to
the older myths—compelled them to seek out
the place. And even more compelling to the college kids were the ghost stories concerning the
long-ago coed, Holly Gayle. He smiled slightly, remembering how he loved to scare Vera with his
own ghostly tales back when they were students at
Stanford. They'd park in woods not so different
from these, and he'd put his arm around her,
making her giggle with delight over the dangers
of The Hook, that hoariest of urban legends,
before reeling her in with more believable tales.

But here . . . Somehow it seemed more dangerous here in these woods than it had where he'd
done his wooing. *Is it really, or am I just an old
man, too close to death to enjoy its threat anymore?*

He rolled the passenger-side window halfway down, to see better. Yes, there was definitely a light, deep in the woods. Greenish, probably due to refractions of light on leaves. *The Greenbriar Ghost is green.* He tried to be amused by the thought, but felt a chill instead. Still, he idled, watching and wondering if he should warn the kids away.

The light winked out. He watched a little longer, one second, two. Silence enveloped him. He realized no crickets chirped, no birds sang. Something had disturbed them—

Suddenly, a dark head appeared, the eyes glowing green pinpricks of light looking at him above the open glass. He gasped as the eyes grew brighter, larger, illuminating the face so that he could see a hint of leaves, a yawn of shadows.

Preternaturally calm, Daniel McCobb was aware of his hand flipping the window switch, rolling it closed, his foot punching the gas pedal. As he drove off, he laughed in delight and disbelief.

23

The Greenbriar Knights were ahead of the Fort Charles Dragons by three points at halftime and Eve's enthusiasm gave her the energy she needed to perform the sets she had learned in the last twenty-four hours. Carried along by the more experienced girls and boosted by her years of practice, she felt confident, even during the tricky Rolling Pyramid routine, which she'd had a terrible time even semimastering in such a small amount of time.

As they came out of it, Heather caught her eye and nodded, giving her a thumbs-up. Eve felt elated as they moved to the side of the field in preparation for the return of the team. The only thing that bothered her was the tattoo. She kept noticing the rose on the rest of the squad's hipbones. *They can't force me to get a tattoo, can they? I won't do it. I can do a decal. Some of those must be decals.*

The Knights, in green tunics, gold pants with green stripes, and golden helmets with green and black shields emblazoned upon them, trotted proudly onto the field. Art Caliban was in the lead, flanked by the other team stars, wide receiver Spencer Lake and Ron Spears, the running back. Eve's eyes danced over their tall broad-shouldered forms and then Art looked her way, grinned, and half waved, half pointed at her. She felt a thrill.

Don't be conceited. Maybe he was looking at somebody else. After all, he was a senior and she was a lowly freshman. Still, that look in his eye . . . She tingled. *Genevieve Camlan, you're imagining things. You can't really even see his eyes under that helmet.*

She didn't care. She *knew*—well, *almost* knew—that he had signaled her.

24

"I kid you not," Daniel McCobb told his wife and son. "I saw the Greenbriar Ghost. In the flesh as it were." He chuckled as he wiped his lips in preparation for a second slice of Vera's succulent pot roast.

"In the flesh, Dad?" Dennis, with his mother's once-auburn hair and the same dark blue eyes, raised an eyebrow, a more paternal trait.

"Yes, in the flesh. I'm sure now that it was a student holding a false head or wearing a mask. There were batteries involved." He shook his head, smiling. "The eyes glowed green and the intensity increased. This wasn't a ten-dollar Halloween mask. This was superb. Why, I nearly wet myself!"

Vera laughed and Dennis, as usual, looked vaguely confused. How they'd had such a straight-arrow boy, Daniel didn't know. Dennis was thirty-two now and still hadn't figured them out. "Son," Danial said, "it's funny. Laugh! Your old man fell for a college prank. A sophomoric one at that!"

"You sound happy about it, Dad."

"Well, I suppose I am. It makes me feel young and naive. Vera, remember the story about the Mt. Sutro phantom I'd tell you about when we were in college?"

His wife blushed. Her laughter tinkled, still music to his ears. "You were such a devil, Danny. Scaring me like that."

Dennis half smiled. "Why'd he scare you?"

"To get into my pants, of course." Vera crinkled up. "More potatoes, honey?"

"Mom, I don't want to hear about that." He held out his plate and she piled on a fresh load.

"You asked," she told him, then passed the gravy and winked at Daniel. "Your father was so good at scaring me, I'm surprised you weren't conceived before we got married."

"Mom! Stop it. That's disgusting."

"All right, Dennis." She looked at Daniel. "Are you sure it was a prank?"

"If it wasn't, I'm either hallucinating or I really did see our mysterious forest elemental."

Vera clapped her hands together. "Oh, Danny, wouldn't that be wonderful, to actually see it after all these years?"

"Doll, it doesn't exist. It's just folklore. Legend."

"You used to think it might be real. You aren't getting all old and stuffy on me, are you, Danny?"

Instead of answering her, he put beef in his

mouth and shut his eyes as he chewed. "Heaven on earth, my doll. How you do it, I don't know, but every time you make this delectable dish, it's better than the last."

"Bosh, you're just easy to please, isn't he, Dennis?"

This, their son understood. "No, Mom. I can't believe how good this is. I miss it."

"You should visit more often. It's only a five-hour drive up from Santo Verde."

"Six, at least. And Jordan hates it when I go away for the weekend."

"She's so jealous!"

"She gets lonely, rambling around in that big house, all alone, all weekend."

"You can bring her."

"You know she hates to travel."

"Bosh, she'd be fine once she got used to it. She's welcome here. And she and Roxie would get along just fine."

"Jordan's a *cat*, Mom."

"I know. Cats and dogs are often friends."

"She's five years old and she's never seen one. They wouldn't get along."

"Nonsense. Roxie would be very nice to her."

"I know. But Jordan's bigger than your little wiener dog. She'd terrorize her."

"You can bring her anyway. She can stay in the guest room with you. I'll make a nice little litter box and she can borrow some of Roxie's dishes."

"I'll think about it." He looked at Daniel. "Dad? Did you really think that the Greenbriar Ghost might exist? Really?"

"I just try to keep an open mind, Dennis. Most legends are based on something real, no matter how far from reality they've strayed."

"What's this one based on?"

"Nature elementals. The green man, primarily. It's also tied in ways to that damned sorority. Their secret society."

"That's still in existence, Danny?" Vera asked. "You haven't mentioned it in years."

"I try not to think about them. But yes, it still exists." *Fata Morgana.* He didn't say the words aloud. "The Gamma sorority president, who is, allegedly, always the leader of the secret society, threw me for a loop when I ran into her the other day. She was nearly a ringer for a president from twenty, twenty-five years ago. Only the hair color didn't match." He felt the chill again, thinking of that young woman.

"Maybe she's the daughter of the former president."

"Could be." Daniel forked food into his mouth, but it had lost some of its flavor. He might tell Vera, but never Dennis, that Malory Thomas and the past president were one in the same. The creature didn't age, and that was how the sorority was tied to the forest elemental. There were sacrifices involved as well. *All legend. It's all just legend.*

He pushed his plate back, and rose. "I'll go make us some coffee."

Vera opened her mouth to tell him she'd do it, then saw his expression and simply nodded.

25

"Ten seconds left on the clock and Art Caliban hands off to Ron Spears. Look at him go! Five seconds as Knights' QB Spencer Lake clears the way—three seconds, two—and touchdown! The Greenbriar Knights win twenty-seven to twenty-one. A great night for some great Knights!"

The cries of the crowd nearly drowned out the announcer and as the squad went into the winning cheers, Eve heard no more. With renewed energy, she picked up her pom-poms and yelled and jumped as the team congratulated itself on the center of the field.

"Okay," Heather said, signaling the squad to stop. "You guys did great! Eve, you were amazing!"

Male voices, laughing and whooping, approached and then the girls were surrounded by big, happy, sweaty men. It was great. "Hey," Art Caliban said, laying a surprisingly gentle hand on her shoulder. She looked up, met his eyes, and smiled, melting inside.

"Hi, Art. Congratulations."

"You want to go get a Coke with me after I clean up?"

"Sure!"

"Now, Art," Heather said, appearing suddenly. "Not tonight. We're taking Eve out ourselves. It's her first night as one of us."

"Heather, you're a mother hen. You can have her some other time. You wouldn't begrudge a returning hero a soda with such a fair maiden, would you?"

A look of displeasure crossed Heather's face so quickly that Eve wasn't sure if she'd imagined it or not. "I guess we should leave it up to Eve. What do you want to do?"

Eve knew exactly what she wanted to do, but was afraid to say so. She looked into Art Caliban's eyes and melted some more, then glanced at Heather and knew she had to go with her sisters. "I'm sorry, Art. Can I have a rain check?"

"You're strong-arming her, Heather, and you know it." Art crossed his arms. He meant business.

Eve felt even more attracted to him, but made herself choose her sisters. "I'm sorry. It's my first night. You know. . . ."

"I know." He put his big arm across her shoulders and gave her a little squeeze. "Go with them tonight. Tomorrow night, we'll go out on a real date. How's that?"

"Sure," Eve agreed, purposely not looking at Heather. "That sounds like fun."

"I'll pick you up at six."

"Great!"

"Where?"

"Where what?"

"Where will I find you?"

"Oh, sorry. At my dorm—"

"No," Heather said. "She'll be all moved into Gamma House by then. You can pick her up there."

"Is that okay?" He smiled.

"It's great!"

"Hi!" Spencer Lake, the quarterback arrived and slapped Art on the back. "Are you moving in on this lady before anyone else has a chance, buddy?"

He smiled at Eve and she felt another warm shiver as a short, obscene vision flashed through her mind. She almost shocked herself with the thought.

"I sure am," Art said, his gaze on Eve. "Better luck next time."

26

The way Heather had acted, Eve half expected that the squad would have some big blowout of a party when they returned to Gamma, still in their uniforms. Instead, two of the subs were sent into the kitchen to fetch glasses and a monstrous pitcher of sweet lemonade. The rest sprawled out on the old comfy furniture in the parlor, sitting up only when the girls returned with the refreshments. Heather had them set the trays on a buffet behind the sofas, then told them to sit down while she did the pouring and serving herself.

Eve thought that was a nice gesture and gratefully took her icy glass, trying to force herself to sip, not chug, the liquid. Her adrenaline had deserted her and now she was glad she hadn't gone out with Art—she was exhausted. She was also relieved when the J-clones drifted upstairs to shower and change. Two had late dates, two were going to bed.

Bed was sounding better by the second. Eve's muscles were beginning to ache and the long hours of practice, combined with the cheering at the game, had drained her last ounce of energy. "I'm going to sleep for a week," she announced. The subs, who had been stationed at either end of the home team's side to lead the crowd in simpler cheers, murmured agreement. Heather and the officers, Teri and Michele, just smiled.

"You'll move in tomorrow," Heather said. "So go back to your dorms and sleep in. We'll expect to see you all tomorrow, with luggage." She rose and walked them out onto the veranda. "Stick together on the walk back to your rooms. Good night."

The night was dark and clear as they set off across the road and started down the sidewalk across the big manicured lawn. There were few students out, considering that it was a Friday night and only half past eleven. "I wonder why Heather told us to stick together," Eve said.

"Maybe because of that dead girl?" little Lou suggested.

"I don't care what they say," chimed in Jelly, who was really Angelica. "I think there's a serial killer in the woods. The trees are close," she added, glancing west, toward the dark forest. "He could be watching us."

"Do you really think so?" Lou asked, picking up her pace.

"Maybe it's the green ghost," suggested Nancy, the other sub.

"Come on," Eve said as they walked even faster.

"That's just an old kids' story. I heard it when I was at cheer camp."

"Yeah," Lou said. "It's silly."

"Okay," Nancy said, "then what about the Gamma ghost? Holly Gayle?"

Eve shivered. "You know about that?"

"My sister was a Gamma. She saw her once."

"Yeah, right," said Jelly.

"Where?" Eve asked.

"In the house. She was just sort of gliding along the second-floor landing. Her feet didn't quite touch the ground. She was dressed in this old-fashioned white dress and her hair looked wet."

"And you believed your sister?" Jelly asked.

"I don't know. I guess not," Nancy admitted. "If I really did believe there was a ghost in Gamma House, I sure as hell wouldn't want to live there."

They crossed another road, nearly at the dorms. "Eve?" Nancy asked.

"Yes?"

"What do you know about the Gamma ghost?"

"Nothing."

"You sounded like you knew something—you seemed surprised I did."

"Well, yeah. I thought that story was pretty obscure. I heard it at camp. Holly was supposed to haunt the lake." She told the truth, simply leaving out what Kendra had told her. It didn't seem like a good idea to repeat all that stuff. *Maybe I'm just afraid to talk about it.* "Here we are," she said as they approached her dorm.

Lou was also in this dorm, while Jelly and Nancy were in a much smaller one next door. They said good night.

Eve entered her room and changed into her robe and slippers, grabbed her pjs and toiletry bag, and headed for the showers down the hall. Every move, now that the adrenaline brought back by the ghost talk had once again deserted her, was forced. She could barely force herself to go through with it; she wanted to turn around and flop on the bed, sweat and all. But she kept going.

The showers were deserted and the large white room with its little stalls echoed her every move, making her nervous. Still, she finally forgot herself under the pounding pulse of the hot water. By the time she dried and dressed for bed, she could barely keep her eyes open, but she didn't ache so much.

It was well after midnight when she finally slipped between cool sheets and set her alarm clock for nine A.M., mere seconds before falling into a deep, dreamless sleep.

27

"Where have you been?" Malory asked when Brittany finally straggled into the windowless ritual room on the second floor of the east wing of Gamma House.

"Sorr-rry!" the girl said, tugging off her clothes unselfconsciously and tossing them against the wall. Nude, Brittany was catnip to cats and bones to dogs, strawberries to cream. Her elemental essence vibrated unfettered throughout the room and harsh words over her tardiness turned mild. Other than masking her true form, Brittany had little magic of her own. Magnetism was her only active art. Animal magnetism—only it wasn't really animal, it was elemental. No one except Malory, and perhaps Heather, really understood the difference. Teri and Michele knew but were too young to comprehend; the rest had no idea she wasn't exactly human.

All of them, even Malory, also not entirely human, were susceptible to her charm if Brittany was nude. Clothing acted like a force field, keeping her charisma from oozing from her pores, preventing people from falling into her thrall.

Humans would interpret what she possessed as a scent, pheromones probably, but it was far more than that. It was beyond definition, part of a sense that had yet to be recognized. It was literally a magnetism, tied to the power of the earth. She was magnetism incarnate and, naked, irresistible.

Naked but for this flesh she had made her own and habitually worn since first teaming with her mistress, she stretched, showing off to the other eleven in the room. All but Malory wore black velvet robes lined with soft forest-green silk; Malory's was green with black silk lining.

Beneath the robes, Brittany knew, they wore nothing. Power was always strongest unencumbered by restrictive clothing; that was true even for humans. The loose robes constricted not at all and actually served to help build up power, holding it in, gathering it, like insulation until the time came to unleash whatever sorcery they were engaged in.

"Where were you?" Malory asked again, trying to refuse the charm. If anyone could, she could.

Brittany smiled, thinking of approaching her, but decided against it; once in Malory's grasp, what power she had was not her own to control anymore. "I was out for a walk in the woods," she lied.

"Really." Malory wasn't buying it. "Did you see him?"

"Him?" Brittany panicked briefly, thinking she meant Professor Tongue. *Guilty, madam.* Then she realized to whom Malory was referring. "No, I didn't see him."

"He's out tonight," her mistress said. "I can feel him. He's impatient. He's hungry."

"I know." Brittany touched her nipples, hardening them. She heard Jenny gasp, looked with amusement at all the younger members of Fata Morgana. Cow eyes, the lot of them, practically drooling, their eyes glued to her. With her charm, her magnetism, she could have any or all of them, even though none but Jenny was gay—and Jenny didn't even know it yet. And Brittany, though genderless when out of body, was now so accustomed to her female flesh that she preferred men most of the time.

"Put your robe on," Malory ordered.

Brittany continued to hesitate.

"I know you weren't in the woods tonight," Malory said. "I was there."

"At the Green Chapel?" Brittany asked innocently.

"Of course."

"I didn't go there."

"You? You can't stay away from the chapel."

"Sure I can. I went for a romp in the woods, to run and climb and look for pine nuts. Only that and nothing more."

Malory eyed her in the way that told Brittany she'd give her no more trouble, so she took her robe off one of the thirteen hooks on the wall and slipped it over her body, then joined the circle of sisters.

"We have three things to discuss. One is initiation rites for Gamma Eta Pi. Since that's not directly Fata Morgana–related and can wait, it shall. Tomorrow, we'll meet here to finalize those plans. No robes necessary for that; we won't be doing magick.

"The two items we must deal with tonight are, of course, preparation of the sacrifice to the Forest Knight, and replacing that bitch Mulva. We need our full circle of thirteen to be at our best." Malory looked from face to face. "I'll take any suggestions you have now."

Brittany knew this was nothing but a game. Malory already had her circle member chosen; there could be no other.

"What about Petra Mills?" Michele said. "She's worthy of sisterhood."

"Yes," Teri agreed.

Malory appeared to consider the idea. "I'm not quite sure about her," she said finally. "You know she takes Prozac. That will dampen any natural power she possesses, and without it, I'm afraid she'd be too depressing to deal with. Any other ideas?"

"Kathryn Whitt?"

"She was raised in a military family. She may have other loyalties that would pop up at inconvenient times. Anyone else?"

She waited a long moment, but no one spoke up. Even the newest members of the circle sensed a decision coming.

"Merilynn Morris," Brittany said. She just couldn't resist.

"Yes. Merilynn Morris," Malory affirmed.

"But she's just a freshman pledge," Heather said.

"Yes, but she holds great power. Haven't you sensed it?" She looked at the others with an expression that seemed to betray amazement at their lack of observational skills.

"She does?" Heather asked. Heather was the ballsiest human here, third in command behind Brittany and Malory herself. "Granted, her eyes seem to show a tie to the forest, but what makes you think she's powerful?"

"Am I ever wrong?"

"No. Well, Mulva disappointed us. You chose her."

"Actually, no, I didn't. She was Brittany's idea. Right, Britt?"

"I'm afraid so," Brittany said smoothly. It was a lie, but that was part of her function as a familiar—to protect her mistress.

"You'll just have to trust me on this, ladies," Malory said. "She's the one."

"But . . ." Michele began.

"But what? Go ahead, you're among friends. I know you're looking out for the welfare of the Fata Morgana."

"Well, the thing is, her uncle raised her from infancy and the man is a Catholic priest."

Malory smiled, eyes sparking merrily. "Yes, that just makes it all the better, don't you think?" She paused. "The girl is not Catholic; she's widely read and, in fact, the priest taught her about all sorts of religions and philosophies. He's not your average pope worshipper."

"And if she doesn't work out, we can always sacrifice her, right, Mal?" Brittany said cheerfully.

Malory looked her up and down. "If it came to that, she'd make a fine sacrifice. And none of you need to worry. I know what I'm doing. I always know."

"So how do we do this?" Michele asked. "She's not even completely initiated into Gamma yet."

"We do that first, of course. Then we'll initiate her into Fata Morgana."

"How do you know she'll want to be a member?"

"Who wouldn't want immortality?"

No one replied; none had been around long enough to be tired of eternal youth yet.

"Very well. Time to perform the rites of sacrifice. Please join hands." She paused. "Tonight we will visit Genevieve Camlan to begin preparing her as a gift to the Forest Knight."

"Does it really have to be Eve?" Heather asked. "I know we agreed, but she's an absolutely fantastic cheerleader. None of the subs can touch her, and I really hate to lose her."

The other cheerleaders murmured agreement.

"Heather, I know," Malory consoled. "And I'm sorry, but it must be. She has the right vibrations, she has power of a sort, and she's a virgin. That old green goat insists on a virgin."

Heather and the pom-pom pushers looked forlorn.

"Don't worry. The fact that she is so dear to you will make her an even better sacrifice. We shall receive many years of grace in exchange for her life. Okay?"

Heather nodded, eyes downcast.

"Good." Malory looked at each girl in turn. "Now, everyone concentrate on sending your power to me so that I can show her the first dream."

Everyone but Malory and Brittany, directly across from her, closed their eyes. Malory began to chant, never breaking the power-inducing gaze she shared with Brittany. After a few moments, the static electricity in the room grew so strong that Brittany could feel her hair trying to lift away from her arms and scalp.

Suddenly, there was an audible *snap* of electricity and all their robes fell from their shoulders. The room swirled with energy; Brittany basked in it, orgasmic with it. She could see the hair rising on the other girls and slowly, she felt gravity lose its grip. Her heels, then toes, left the ground.

"Genevieve," Malory said. "What scares you, Genevieve?"

She closed her eyes and Brittany saw that her mistress had already divined the answer to that question.

28

Eve awoke in blackness, the dark wet smell of the lake overwhelming her senses. She lay paralyzed, suffocated by silence.

I'm dead.

No. You're dreaming.

She tried to reach for the bedside lamp, but her arms wouldn't obey. She squinted into the darkness but discerned nothing except a slight cool breeze on her cheek, a breeze scented by lake water, an odor of wet stones and moss, a vague scent of violets beneath it, like musty old cologne.

Where am I?

Her tiny dorm room had a window and normally she could see the yellow glow of one of the tall sodium lights that guarded the entrances to the building. But now it was blotted out; everything was lost to perfect blackness, so thick she could feel it pressing against her.

And then a voice, a murmur so soft it seemed almost to be within her head. "Genevieve."

Who's there?

It's me, Eve. Remember me?

It was a feminine voice, but Eve didn't recognize it. She strained to move, but invisible ropes seemed to hold her to the bed. Still, she could not speak. *No. I don't remember you. Who are you? What do you want?*

High-pitched laughter tinkled down the scale. *We met a long time ago.*

Where? Terror filled Eve; she felt as if her heart would stop.

You've hurt my feelings. You know me. You've seen me. Then tell me who you are.

You saw me on Applehead Island a long time ago.

Eve suddenly wished to die; she couldn't take the terror she felt now. *The green ghost,* she thought.

There was a pause.

"Damn," Malory murmured, "I thought she was afraid of Holly Gayle." She smiled. "This is better."

So you remember me now?

As she heard the words, the voice began to deepen.

Eve saw a pair of glowing green eyes blink to life. Slowly, they moved closer to the bed.

Genevieve, you remember me now, don't you?

Eve told herself it was a dream. Just a dream. The paralysis wouldn't break. She tried to scream, but she couldn't open her mouth; it seemed sewed shut.

It's not a dream, Eve. I'm here, to visit you.

Go away! Please, go away!

The eyes stared down at her, right at the bedside now. *You're afraid, aren't you, little Eve? Afraid of me?*

Lake water seemed to drench her. *Please go away! You're not real!*

The laugh came again, now masculine. *Here's how real I am, Eve.*

The eyes lowered toward her. Eve tried to shut her own, but nothing happened. She couldn't look away. *It's a dream. It's a dream. Wake up! Wake up right now!*

The eyes moved until they were directly in front of her face, only inches from her own. Emerald-green fire with slitted pupils, they blinked slowly. *Genevieve, you're mine.*

She felt cold breath from the mouth she couldn't see. It was dank and icy against her face. *Go away!*

A cold, slimy tongue touched her chin, then licked upward, over her left cheek, across her forehead, slowly, so slowly, and then down her right cheek, back to her chin. It left a cold snail trail in its wake.

No!

Yes! The tongue wiggled across her lips, probing, entering her mouth, licking the insides of her lips, tasting her teeth.

Saliva, cold thick gel, tasting of lake water and earth, oozed into her mouth. She opened her mouth to scream and though there was no sound, her teeth parted. The tongue, like a piece of raw chicken cold from the refrigerator, pushed into her mouth, examining her tongue, her molars, running along her gums.

Stop it!

"Damn it!" Malory said again, this time breaking the spell.

Gravity pulled at their toes, drawing them back down an inch, so that their feet were solidly on the floor. Electric hair settled. Tension left the room.

"What happened?" Heather asked.

Malory laughed lightly. "The bad news is, I lost her. The good news is that she was so frightened, she fainted."

29

Eve first awoke to darkness, confused and afraid, unable to remember what happened. *A nightmare? I must have had a nightmare.*

She turned her head and looked toward the window, vague relief flooding her as she spied the outline of the frame, the Roman shade left half up. Beyond the glass, the street lamp cast an amber glow. Then she noticed the funny taste in her mouth.

No, not a funny taste. A bad taste. A *horrible* taste.

She reached out and touched the bedside lamp. It glowed dimly. She tapped it again to bring more light, then sat up, moving her tongue against the roof of her mouth, touching her teeth. *Disgusting.* The dream came back, a harsh jolt. The tongue licking her face, invading her mouth, leaving snail trails of cold slime behind.

She jumped out of bed, gagging, fumbled with the chain lock, and opened her door. The dimly lit hall was deserted. She raced to the closest rest room and paused in front of the sinks and mirrors just long enough to see the sticky glistening tracks on her face. "Dear God." she whispered. "It really happened!"

She barely made it into a stall before she lost the contents of her stomach. There wasn't much to throw up, but she couldn't stop. The harsh acidic dregs of lemonade burned her throat with every heave.

Gasping, she finally stood up, flushed, and left the toilet. At the sink she used her hands as a cup, repeatedly swishing water through her mouth and spitting it out. Finally, she scrubbed her face in water too hot to be good for her complexion, but she didn't care; all she wanted to do was get the feeling of filth off her skin.

Back in her room, she turned on the overhead light and sat on her bed, trying to figure out what happened. It felt like a dream—but that slime on her face, in her mouth. It must have been real. Had someone broken in?

The alarm clock read four-thirty. She rose and began searching the room for signs of an intruder. She stopped, her eyes on the door. The chain latch. She'd slipped it in place when she came home and she'd undone it when she ran to the rest room. No one could have been in the room. *Unless* . . .

Remembering the hidden panel Malory had used at Gamma House, she examined the walls of her room, but there was nothing to find in the little shoe box of a bedroom. The building was modern and the off-white plaster walls weren't capable of hiding any mysteries.

So it had to be a dream. What else could it be?

Slightly less nervous, but leaving the overhead light on, Eve slipped back into bed and turned on her side to keep the light from shining directly in her eyes. Staring in the direction of the door, she thought more about what could have happened and eventually decided that something she ate had disagreed with her digestive system, causing her to produce lots of nasty saliva herself. That made sense. *I was so tired that when I got nauseated, I didn't even wake up. Instead it made me dream.*

Slowly, her eyes closed and the next time she woke up, the sun was up, the sky clear and blue outside her window.

30

"I know what you showed Eve last night," Brittany said as she painted her toenails.

"Of course you do," Malory replied, brushing her dark hair in long, even strokes. "What else is new?"

Brittany paused, looking at her mistress. "The dream you sent her was very interesting. That astral form of the Forest Knight was something else."

"It really drew a lot of energy," Malory replied. "Almost more than the girls could handle. We have to get our thirteenth member installed right away."

"Yes, I know. But, Malory, what about the astral form? You added a new twist."

Malory blinked slowly. "What was a new twist?"

"Don't tease me. You know. Do I have to say it?"

"Of course you do."

"The tongue. I want to know the inspiration for it."

Malory half smiled. "You know the inspiration for it. Intimately. Frankly, what made me think of it was your tardiness."

"What?"

"I know where you were last night. Under Piccolo's tongue. Shame on you."

"I never—"

"Oh, don't bother. We both know you did."

"Why is it all right for you to visit him alone, but not me?"

"Those are the rules."

"I'm tired of the rules."

"You shouldn't be. You break them often enough."

Was she bluffing? Brittany couldn't tell, but she had thought that Malory rarely realized what she was up to. She capped her nail polish and stretched out on her mistress's wide bed.

"Brittany? Haven't you anything to say?"

"I do *not* break the rules. Hardly ever. I wouldn't lie to you."

Malory whirled and crossed the room so quickly that even Brittany, as quick as she was, couldn't avoid being pinned against the bed. "You lie frequently," Malory said, her face only inches above Brittany's.

"Watch out—you'll smear my nail polish." She lifted her head and planted a quick kiss on Malory's lips. "I'm your most faithful companion," she said softly. "You know that."

"You're also my most horny companion."

"Thank you."

"That wasn't a compliment."

"It felt like one." She kissed her again, trying

to charm her. *Damned clothes, always getting in the way.*

Malory's nostrils flared, her voice softened, and she brought her face closer to Brittany's, traveling down to her neck, then up by one ear, taking in her scent. "I know what you're doing."

It's working. "I'm not doing anything, mistress. You're the one on top."

"Yes, I am. Remember that. I'm always on top. Don't play with my toys behind my back. That includes Professor Tongue." She sat up, keeping Brittany pinned beneath her. "Promise."

"I promise." Brittany reached up to touch Malory's breasts.

"None of that. You're off the hook and we have work to do. It's moving day. The pledges will start showing up soon." She swung away, freeing Brittany. "Get up and get busy."

"What do you want me to do?"

"Make sure all the sisters in the west wing have clean rooms. We want the pledges to be impressed."

"Okay." Brittany got up and slipped her feet into sandals, then grabbed a half-empty yellow bag of Peanut M&Ms and headed for the door.

"Britt?"

She turned, her hand on the knob. "Yes?"

"Be good. Maybe later I'll take you to the professor's house with me."

Brittany smiled and blew her a kiss, then left Malory's room. The biggest in the east wing, it was more like a hotel suite, with a small living area, walk-in closets, and a luxurious bathroom. It had been luxurious before they returned to Greenbriar after their stint running a Gamma House in Vermont, but Malory had it remodeled three years ago to include a whirlpool and all new furniture, paint, and fixtures. Only Brittany was allowed extended visits. The other Fata Morganas had seen the room occasionally, but never the ordinary sisters.

She crossed the stair landing and walked into the west wing and knocked on the first door.

"Come in," called a sister.

Brittany entered, chirped a greeting around the M&M she sucked on. The room was nice, a single, but it was only a bedroom glorified with nice furniture. This sister shared an adjoining bath with the next single room, which seemed pretty great if you didn't know that Malory's digs took up at least five times the space, not counting her private bathroom and walk-in closet. And the Fata Morganas' single rooms were all twice the size of this one, each with its own private bathroom. Malory was right about not letting the simpler sisters see how they lived in the east wing.

This sister, the newest one, barely out of pledgehood, looked at Brittany questioningly. "What's up?"

What's her damned name? "You have a nice room," she said, glancing around. Her eyes landed on the girl's desk. A copy of the school paper, the *Greenbriar Herald,* lay on top, open to a story about a possible food poisoning incident in the school cafeteria. The byline told her what she needed to know. *Samantha Penrose.*

"Samantha, I just wanted to let you know that the pledges will start drifting in soon."

"Just Sam, please." Just Sam stared at her expectantly. "Is there something I should do?"

"Do? No. Just answer questions if you're around, okay?"

"No problem. Maybe I'll ask some too."

"What? What do you mean?"

"You know I write for the *Herald.* I saw you got my name off the paper."

"No—"

"It's all right. You have to remember a lot of names." She smiled. "Maybe I'll see if I can get some good comments and do a story about the pledges' moving day."

"Oh, sure, I guess. Maybe you should check with Malory."

"Why?"

Brittany didn't like the look in this one's eye. "She's in charge," she said. "Everybody checks everything with Malory."

"I see."

"Okay, see you later."

"See you."

Brittany left the room, closing the door behind her. How had Sam Penrose become a Gamma? *A brain, destined to edit the paper. We could use a good journalist on our side. Now and in the future.* She nodded to herself, remembering Malory's words. It made sense, but it didn't make her like the girl any better. Still, Malory knew best. Usually.

She knocked on the next door. No one replied, so she let herself in—regular sisters didn't get to lock their doors; it was part of the trust-and-loyalty thing Malory kept beating into them. Brittany rifled through the absent sister's desk and dresser. Of course, the lack of locks was for Malory's benefit. *And mine.* She fished a shiny red thong from the drawer. It looked to be her size. Quickly, she checked the crotch. *Doesn't look dirty.* She sniffed it. *Doesn't smell dirty.* In fact, it smelled brand-new. She tucked it into her jeans, closed the drawer, and went on about her appointed rounds.

31

Kendra Phillips set her computer monitor on her desk. "There," she said. "That's the last of my stuff. I'm officially out of the dorm, I guess."

"You *guess?*" Eve asked. "This room is huge! It's probably five times the size of my dorm room. That was nothing but a walk-in closet. This is so nice and airy!"

"I had a roommate at the dorm, and I'll tell you, a double over there was just a one-and-a-half. I could barely breathe. My roommate was an idiot. And she snored. She'd wake me up sometimes making these funny little 'wee-wee-wee' snorts. 'Wee-wee-wee, all the way home.'" She shook her head. "I sure won't miss that."

Eve smiled, but didn't speak. She seemed to be concentrating on neatly placing pair after pair of underwear in her chest of drawers.

"So, do you snore?" Kendra prodded.

"What? Oh, no! I mean, I don't think so. Oh—"

"Eve, don't be so serious. I'm teasing you."

"I don't think I snore."

"I don't think I do either, but if I do, you just poke me and tell me to turn over." She watched Eve. "I can't read you. You're overjoyed to be moving in here, but you're all weird and serious. What's up? And is there any color of panties that you *don't* have?"

Eve smiled again. "I don't have red ones."

"Why not?"

"I don't like red underwear."

"I know what you mean. Reminds you of your first period, doesn't it?"

Eve's jaw dropped. "No! Ewww! Gross!"

Kendra collapsed onto a small empty spot on her bed, laughing helplessly.

"What?" Eve asked.

Kendra couldn't answer.

Eve watched her. "You were kidding? That was a joke?"

"Yes, I was joking." Her words sputtered among her laughs. "Girl, you are the most gullible thing I've ever met."

"No, I'm not. I mean, it was logical."

"Spotty."

"What?"

"Spotty. That's what I got called for the last half of my freshman year. Fortunately, those girls in gym class didn't remember to start calling me that again the next year."

"They called you that? Because—"

"Because of a couple little spots. I didn't realize I wasn't, well, protected as well as I should have been. I didn't know until they started yelling it at me in the locker room."

"That's awful. Like *Carrie*."

"Evie, you don't know how right you are. They'd seen that movie and they pelted me with tampons." She smiled. "At least they weren't used!"

"Gross." Eve hesitated. "Were you—did you have a hard time in high school? I mean—"

"Was I a loser, a nerd? No, not really. It just happened that the girls I shared a locker room with were a bunch of cliquey bitches. They all had nicknames for each other. Spice, Sugar, Brown Sugar, Vanilla, Nutmeg, and Limey. I'll never forget those nicknames."

"*Limey?*" Eve gasped. "What was wrong with her? Jaundice?"

"Sweetie, it's not *all* about color! She was British."

"Oh."

"Actually, most of the names were about color, now that I think about it. But not like you think. Brown Sugar was white and spent all her free time in a tanning bed. Sugar was Latina, Vanilla was African-American but thought she was white. She was an Oreo."

"What do you mean?"

"Vanilla loved country music. And no self-respecting black girl does the Texas two-step, except Vanilla. She did. She even got them to do some cowboy-style cheerleading. It was hysterical, but everybody loved it."

"Wait a minute," Eve said. "You mean the girls that called you that awful name were *cheerleaders?*"

"I'm afraid so." She smiled. "You won't call me 'Spotty' though, will you?"

"Of course not!"

Kendra grinned.

"You're teasing again," Eve said firmly. "You know I wouldn't ever call you that. I think it's awful. I feel like I should apologize to you on behalf of good cheerleaders everywhere."

"As opposed to evil cheerleaders?"

Eve hesitated, then smiled broadly. "Yeah, why not?"

"To be completely fair, that clique wasn't evil, even if most of them were airheads. They nicknamed everybody they liked. Some of their friends had names just as bad as 'Spotty.' It was probably a compliment."

"If it was, it was a bad one. I have to admit that some cheerleaders really are major airheads, totally full of themselves."

"Hanging all over the football players." Kendra started to chuckle, then stopped herself, seeing the look on Eve's face. "What did I just say? You're as red as a radish."

"I have a date tonight," Eve said softly. "With the captain of the Greenbriar Knights."

"Oh! Lord, I stuck my foot in my mouth so far they'll need the jaws of life to get it out again. I didn't mean—"

"Of course not." Gradually, Eve began smiling.

"I know the girls you mean. The power freaks. They're only interested in a guy they can show off. They don't care anything about the guy. They only care about what he looks like and what his rep around school is."

"He's a trophy," Kendra added, to spur Eve on, to bring her out of whatever had put her in a funk.

"Exactly. And there are girls who are twice as bad."

"Which ones are those?"

"The ones who steal your boyfriend. Those bitches only want a guy because he's spoken for . . . and because he's a big deal on campus."

"Sounds like you've experienced one of those bitches."

"Yes. More than once."

"Let me guess. You were head cheerleader?"

Eve nodded.

"And your boyfriend was on the football team?"

"Yes. One was the captain." Her lips crooked up wryly.

"Shit, Evie," Kendra said. "Then you were just asking for it."

Finally, Eve chuckled with her. "I guess so. You know, I didn't think about it when I accepted the date with Art—I hope he doesn't have a girl-friend."

"You didn't get here early enough to hear the local gossip. Art Caliburn has never been ensnared in any romances, nor has his buddy the running back—"

"Spencer Lake."

"Yeah. Spencer." Kendra licked her upper lip suggestively. "You know, Spence looked pretty tasty. For a jock. Think you can fix me up—okay, what did I say now?"

"Nothing. You didn't say anything wrong."

"Do you just turn colors for no reason? Now you're doing your ghost impression again. What'd I do? Are you crying?" Not waiting for a reply, she crossed to the door and shut it, then put an arm around Eve and led her to the bed, sat her down, then made room for herself next to her.

"Okay, Evie," she said, taking one of her hands in both her own. "Look at me. Are you crying?"

"No."

"Then why are you shaking?"

"I'm not."

"You're lying. I can *feel* you shaking."

Eve tried to pull her hand away, but Kendra wouldn't allow it. "Look, we're stuck with each other for the duration, Evie, and you have to tell me how I upset you, or I'll never stop. You'll be turning all sorts of colors every time I open my mouth, and I'll just keep making you cry—"

"I'm not crying." Eve finally met her gaze.

"Well, then, what's that stuff running down your face if it's not tears? Oh, shit. *Now* what did I do?"

"You didn't *do* anything. You said something

this time. God, I'm acting like such an idiot!"
Eve's voice trembled, but there was a giggly tone
to it that belied the fresh crop of tears.

Kendra switched from hand-holding to a hug,
a hard one. "Eve, listen to me. You're going to
get hysterical if you don't get a grip right now."

Eve sobbed a giggle.

Kendra decided slapping her face would be a
bad idea. Instead, she took her shoulders in both
hands and forced her to turn toward her. "Control yourself. If you don't, you'll attract attention
and that gossip group I told you about will be
gossiping about *you*. Now, take a deep breath.
Good. Exhale. Another breath. Hold it. Exhale."

The fourth deep inhalation did the trick.
Kendra handed her a tissue and Eve wiped away
the tears from her cheeks and the hysteria from
her eyes. A small giggle escaped, but it sounded
normal.

"So, are you one of those high-maintenance
girls, Evie?"

"No. I'm so sorry. I can just imagine what you
think of me. I was being so stupid—"

"Stop calling yourself stupid. Do you know
how often you do that?"

"No."

"You do it a lot. You're not stupid."

"I do lots of stupid things."

"No. You're not stupid and I don't ever want
to hear you saying that again. I'm going to inter-
rupt you if you say it until you learn not to. Evie,

you're smart. And you're gullible as hell, but you've got me now."

"What do you mean?"

"I'll teach you to be a first-class bullshit detective."

For a second, she thought Eve was going to cry again, but the girl sat up straighter and quickly dashed away the tears welling in her eyes. "That's the sweetest thing anyone ever said to me, Kendra. Thank you." With that, she hugged back, long and warm.

What have *I gotten myself into?* Kendra felt a little teary herself, mired in all this warm sentimental goo that she herself had somehow stirred up. She stroked Eve's hair, then pulled gently from the hug. *An egghead and a cheerleader, who would've thought?*

"Okay. Now, tell me what I did and what I said. Leave nothing out."

"It's stupid—"

"What'd I tell you?"

"Sorry. But, well, okay. It's embarrassing. I had a nightmare. . . ."

32

At three o'clock, all the sisters, old and new, of Gamma Eta Pi met in the drawing room, and this time, the pledges were assigned to wheel in the extra chairs and set them up. And this time, Brittany informed them in her chirpy little voice, they got the cheap seats while the more senior sisters took the upholstered furniture.

Eve unfolded several chairs, very aware of Kendra sticking close, like a mama lion. She'd never experienced the kind of understanding that her new roommate offered her, nor the warmth. After she told her the details of the horrible dream about the slimy tongue, Kendra told her about a tribe of Australian aboriginals who taught their children to control their dreams, to call their parents into their dreams for help, then invited Eve to call on her the same way.

No one had ever treated her this way, not her friends or even her parents. They were great parents, but they tended to worry a lot about what other people thought of their family, of their home, their career status. Eve never would have dared repeat the dream to her mother or any of the friends she'd made since she became a cheerleader long before high school. Her mother would have told her not to let her imagination run away with her, her friends would have laughed.

"Eve?" someone asked.

She turned and came eye to eye with Merilynn Morris. "Hi."

"Do you remember me now?" Merilynn asked.

"Uh, from camp, right?" She forced herself to maintain eye contact. Sensing Kendra standing slightly behind her left shoulder gave her an added boost.

"Yes, from camp. Don't tell me you've forgotten about our adventures."

Eve hesitated. Merilynn, slender and smaller in every way, was still beautiful in a Renaissance painting sort of way. The brilliant green eyes, long and slightly hooded, pinned her, but they were nothing like the monster eyes she'd dreamed up the previous night. They were friendly, but faraway, as if their owner always had one foot in the clouds—and as far as Eve could recall, that was accurate.

Her face was more round than oval, but on her it looked good. Her mouth was long, like her eyes, the lips neither narrow nor full. The corners tilted up, by genetic design or habit, Eve didn't know, but either way, it worked. As she studied her, she kept thinking of a painting she'd seen prints of several times. It was a portrait of a

woman with long tendrils of bright auburn hair
and she wore a gown shaded in golds and fiery
oranges. Her eyes were green and she appeared
serene yet amused, much like the Mona Lisa, but
prettier and happier and far more colorful. Eve
had always been drawn to the painting, though
looking at it made her slightly uneasy. Seeing
Merilynn now, she finally understood why. They
were nearly twins, though Merilynn's eyes were
more startling and a faint spray of freckles over
her nose and cheeks gave her an impish look.

"Hello," Kendra said, extending her hand.
"I'm Eve's roommate, Kendra Phillips."

"Merilynn Morris. I'm pleased to meet you.
Eve? Have you forgotten our adventures?"

Eve told herself to smile. "I'm sorry. I really
don't remember all that much—I haven't thought
of it in years. I mean, well, I went to Applehead
every year, not just once, so there are lots of things
to remember."

Merilynn smiled widely and dimples appeared.
Eve had forgotten she had them. She looked
more elfin than ever. "Of course. I liked Applehead—I loved being there, on that lake—but I
didn't have any talent for cheerleading. Father
just thought I might like to try it. He told me all
those old ghost stories." Eyes twinkling, she
added, "I didn't know the ghost of Holly Gayle is
supposed to walk the halls of Gamma though. I
thought she was a lake spirit."

Eve swallowed panic. Merilynn was doing

exactly what she feared she'd do: dredging up old nightmares. "So, how's your father these days?"

"He's great. Aging beautifully. Too bad he's celibate. He'd be a real chick magnet."

"Your father is celibate?" Kendra asked.

"He's a Catholic priest," Eve said.

"See, you remember me!"

"Not everybody has a priest for a dad."

"How did *that* happen?" Kendra moved closer.

"My parents died when I was a baby. Father is really my uncle Martin. My father's brother."

"I remember you said you thought he might be your real dad. Do you still think so?"

Merilynn shrugged. "I was just a kid. You know how kids are. So how come you remember all that stuff but not our trip out to the island?"

"I remember we did it." Eve shifted uncomfortably, hoping the meeting would be called to order. "It rained. We barely got back before everybody got back from the field trip." She glanced at Kendra and knew she didn't have to worry about her spilling the story about the island she'd told her when they first met.

"Do you remember what we saw?"

"We spooked ourselves, making up stories."

Merilynn paused, then barely nodded. "We sure did. Have you talked to Sam Penrose yet?"

"No."

"You remember her though?"

"Sure. She always made me nervous."

"Really?" Merilynn smiled at Kendra. "Sam went on our adventures too. She's already a full sister here. Can you imagine *her* joining a sorority?"

I can't imagine you joining a sorority. Or why you had to choose this one. "Gamma's really good for careers, and she was the most driven person I've ever met."

"She still is. She's going to be a journalist. The serious kind. I guarantee you that girl will bust open government scandals in the future. Or maybe she'll be a war correspondent."

"She'll probably do both," Eve said. "I've never met anybody braver."

"Sam Penrose sounds very imposing." Kendra chuckled. "I don't know if I want to meet her or not."

"Too late," Merilynn said, waving at someone who just came into the room. "Sam, come here!"

"Hello, Merilynn."

"Sam Penrose, meet Kendra Phillips, and I think you already know Eve Camlan."

Sam shook hands with both of them, then looked Eve up and down. "You're drop-dead gorgeous. I always thought you would be."

"Thanks. You look great too." *Great but scary.* She was of average size, but somehow she came off as tall and imposing. She still had her straight-backed, square-shouldered posture, her figure hidden beneath a black tank top and an oversize blue broadcloth shirt, the sleeves rolled up to her elbows. Her face was strong, with dark, perfectly arched eyebrows over dark eyes. Prominent cheek-bones offset her square chin. Her sable hair was much better kept now, sleek with a biometric cut that let it shape naturally into a below–the–chin bob. The youthful Sam had had no interest in hair, but puberty must have tamed the tomboy within. "I love your hair," Eve said with complete sincerity.

"Thanks." Sam's left eyebrow shot up in a question mark. Eve had forgotten about that too. It was the "you are an alien, please explain" look she'd seen back at camp so many times. It made her think of Mr. Spock.

"Where do you get it cut?"

"That place in Caledonia on Main Street."

"Everything's on Main Street in Caledonia," Kendra noted.

"The little place between Java the Hut and the dildo store. Has a cute name."

"Everything in Caledonia—" Kendra began.

"—has a cute name," they finished in unison. Eve was amused, mainly because the smile that passed between the two young women made her a little jealous. She knew it was silly. Kendra was just the sort of person Sam would get along with. Another brain with balls.

"The dildo store?" Merilynn asked.

"The Marital Aide Museum and Emporium," Kendra explained.

"That's the name." Sam rubbed the faint cleft

in her chin and peered briefly at the ceiling. "It's something like Hair Today, Gone Tomorrow."

Kendra cracked up, which signaled Eve that the serious journalist had made a joke. She hadn't known Sam had a sense of humor and because of that, she hadn't zoned in on the goofy name. She'd taken it seriously. Maybe Sam wasn't as bad as she'd thought.

"Sam, Eve doesn't remember much about our adventures."

"Which adventures?"

"At Applehead Island, for one."

"We rowed out there, goofed off, and rowed back in a rainstorm. We nearly got caught. It was fun."

"What, you don't remember what we saw?" Merilynn asked, eyes wide.

Up went the eyebrow. Sam glanced toward the fireplace. "The meeting is starting. We'll talk more later." She left the pledges to sit with the full sisters.

"Hmmph," Merilynn said. "I guess you're both in denial."

"The meeting will come to order," called out Malory Thomas.

Eve sat down, grateful to Kendra for deftly maneuvering herself into a chair that would separate her from Merilynn.

33

"I hope all the Gamma meetings won't be that long and boring," Kendra told Eve as soon as they got back to their room and shut the door.

Eve rolled her eyes. "It was awful!" She tossed the booklet of Gamma House rules and history on her desk. "I don't know what pisses me off most. That we have to be in before eleven tonight or that we have to practically memorize that rule book because they're going to test us. I *hate* tests. I freeze."

"We'll study together. We'll make it fun."

"You like to study?"

"Not this stupid book." Kendra tossed hers on her bed. "I've got enough real studying to do. Way too much. I shouldn't have taken so many credits this semester. It's just too much. Look at that stack of books on my desk." She indicated a solid foot and a half of texts. "I have to write two papers and read chapters out of every book in that stack. Before Monday."

"Why don't you drop a class or two?" Eve slid

her closet open and started looking through her wardrobe for something to wear on her date.

"Are you kidding? I wouldn't know what to drop. I managed to get into ones I didn't think I would. I can't drop those—they're interesting."

"What about Piccolo's class?"

"It's easy, and I'd have to pick it up again later if I dropped it now. I'd rather get it over with. Besides, we have it together three days a week and it's just before lunch."

Eve laughed. "Don't drop it." She pulled a cobalt-blue dress from the closet and held it up. "What do you think?"

"It's gorgeous. A little dressy, probably."

"You're right." Eve replaced the dress and continued searching. "So what do you know about Professor Piccolo? Something's going on with him."

"You mean all those girls who are moony for him?"

"Yeah. I mean, he's *old,* but not all that good looking. He's just average."

"I think he's not average in *one* department."

Eve whirled around, holding up a lavender dress with a ruffled neckline.

"Too floofy. Way too floofy. I'd throw that one out if I were you."

"What's floofy mean?"

"You know—puffy and too sweet. Stuff that makes you look like you should be working in the Enchanted Castle at Disneyland."

"Oh." Eve looked the dress over. She loved it, but Kendra was right. She hung it up at the far end of the closet, then turned back to Kendra. "So Piccolo's packing a giant dingus?" She giggled.

"Is there anything that doesn't make you blush?" Kendra asked in mock annoyance. "Actually, I don't think they're talking penis, but where did you ever get a word like 'dingus'?"

"That's not a regular word?"

"I never heard it used that way before."

"Oh? That's what my mother calls them." She snickered and blushed again. "Dinguses. There's some old movie called *Dirty Dingus McGee* and my mother would just fall apart when she heard the title. My dad said it a lot. I asked her why it was funny, but she didn't tell me until I was thirteen. Her mother called it a 'dingus' too." She laughed. "So I guess it's a family heirloom."

"Dingus. It's growing on me."

"Eww!" Eve giggled, blushing madly.

"So, little Miss Innocence, you get the nasty jokes fast."

Eve grinned and held up a summery white halter-topped dress.

"Nope. Way too Marilyn Monroe. People will think you're a drag queen."

"Hey!"

"Not really."

"Thank you."

"You don't have an Adam's apple."

"You're messing with me."

"Yep." Kendra joined her at the closet and started pawing through the clothes.

"I don't have a fourth as much in my wardrobe as you do. This is amazing. I'm surprised they all fit in here."

"You can borrow whatever you want."

"That's sweet of you."

"So what isn't average about Piccolo if it isn't his dingus?"

"Well, I haven't heard much yet, but rumor has it he can lick his own forehead. Of course, if he could do that, he'd be a freak of nature." She laughed. "And being a guy, he'd probably spend all his time licking himself."

Eve's giggles faded after a few seconds. "You mean he has a huge *tongue*?"

Kendra looked her in the eye. "Yeah. I purposely didn't use that word. Because of your nightmare."

"It's a pretty weird coincidence."

"But that's all it is."

"I know. And I'm pretty much over the tongue dream. Telling you got it out of my system."

"Good. So I'll tell you the rest. He has a nickname."

"What is it?"

"Professor Tongue. And I don't know if it's true or not, but I heard he's currently servicing President Malory."

"Really?"

Kendra nodded as she pulled forth a sleek pair of black pants. "Wear these."

"With what?"

"Depends. Are you a first-timer?"

"How'd you know?"

"I didn't. I didn't really think you'd say yes. I mean, with all that blushing and words like 'dingus,' and all, I was starting to think you're a virgin."

"I am. That's not what you meant?"

"Lord, no. I meant, do you ever have sex on a first date?"

Eve's eyes widened. "Of course not! I've never gone all the way!"

"Saving it for your wedding night?"

"No, just for the right guy."

"Okay, so, how do we dress a virgin for a first date?"

"Don't tell anyone!"

"Of course not. Did you hear me ratting you out to Merilynn about that island adventure you pretended not to remember?"

"I'm sorry. I'm not used to trusting other females."

"But you're a cheerleader. You have all those bonds with other women."

"Which is why I don't usually trust them."

"I'm curious. Do you trust Merilynn? I know you don't want to be around her, but would you trust her?"

"Honestly? No. She's a little scary."

"She and Sam Penrose both scare you?"

"Totally different scaries," Eve explained. "Sam is like royalty or something. She commands. She keeps people together. I doubt we'd have gotten off that island in that storm without her. She never loses her head." She paused. "Of course, we probably wouldn't have gotten there without her, either. She figured out when and how to do it without getting caught. She made it happen."

"So she doesn't actually *frighten* you?"

"No. But I don't like being around her—she's just so intense. Actually, she's a lot like you, but without a personality."

"Is that a compliment?"

"Yes."

"I thought so. She's got a personality, but you're right. She intimidates people. I doubt if she even realizes it consciously. She'll have to figure it out to make it as a journalist. She'll have to learn to tone it down when she needs to."

"At least Gamma's the right place to do it."

"Yeah. All that stuff about teaching us all about reading body language and decoding the way people use words—that's going to be cool. Lessons like that are hard to come by."

"No wonder this sorority has so many successful alumni."

"Here." Kendra handed her a black tank top. "Wear this."

"All black? It's hot out. And I'm not really the all-black type. Or do you mean I should just wear the pants and top, nothing over it?"

"Nope." Kendra returned to the closet. "I saw the perfect thing in here somewhere. Tell me how Merilynn is scary."

"She's impetuous. She thinks of something and runs off and does it without thinking about consequences. And she's probably still into all that witchy stuff."

"I wouldn't trust her either—she seems a little flaky. But she's into witchcraft? Wicca?"

"I don't know. She always knew about all sorts of occult things. She liked to mess with herbs and hold séances and things like that."

"Well, that doesn't make her flaky. A lot of that stuff is pretty legitimate. I think her flakiness is probably just an inborn trait. Like Sam should be an army general. Or maybe a conductor."

"On a train?"

Kendra laughed. "No, no! I mean an orchestra conductor."

Eve smiled. "So I guess being a cheerleader is my inborn trait. What's yours?"

Kendra had never thought about it before, but she instantly answered. "I'm a storyteller. Old stories, not new ones. Aha. Here." She took a lightweight pale pink jacket from its hanger and handed to Eve. "I assume you have jewelry of some sort that has pink in it."

"I do. It's a pendant. A heart carved out of pink crystal."

"Perfect. You'll look great." She paused, watching Eve look over the outfit she'd picked out.

"You don't have to wear that. I mean, you probably know lots more about clothes than I do."

"Probably, but this is interesting. I've never worn this jacket with black before. I always wear pastels with it."

"You should wear whatever makes you feel good."

"I think this might make me feel good," Eve said, kicking off her shoes.

Kendra sat down at her desk and started picking through the textbooks. "Well, while you're out having a good time, I'm going to work on my paper for Professor McCobb's class. At least it's interesting. It's on modern American iconography."

"Translation?" Eve's voice was muffled behind her clothing.

"The immortality of Elvis Presley, for instance. He was a real person, but he's turning into a modern folk hero."

"That *is* interesting. Okay. How's this look?"

Kendra turned. Eve had completely dressed, right down to the pendant, in under a minute. "Amazing."

"You like it, then."

"I love it. It makes you look more mature, which is good when you're dating a senior. But what's amazing is how fast you changed clothes."

"Being a cheerleader teaches you to be a quick-change artist." She moved to the mirror of the dresser they shared, quickly brushing her hair and applying makeup.

Kendra watched in fascination. "You've got to teach me how to do that."

"Do what?" Eve asked, dropping her lipstick in a small black shoulder bag.

"Put on makeup that fast. It takes me forever."

Someone knocked on the door.

"Art," Kendra said.

Eve smiled and opened the door, but it wasn't Art Caliban.

Heather smiled at her. "Art's waiting for you in the foyer. And guess what?"

"What?"

"He's taking you to Thai Gonzales. My date and I are going there too, so we're going to double-date. Won't that be fun?"

Eve shot a grimace to Kendra that spoke of slow death and torture. "What is Thai Gonzales?" she asked brightly.

"It's a nice little restaurant in Greenbriar. Since we have to be back early, it's the perfect choice."

"Oh?"

"They serve Thai and Mexican food. You can get just one or a combo. The cuisines use some of the same spices. Cilantro. Red pepper. Cumin. They're really good mixed. You'll love it." Heather flashed her teeth. "You ready? Let's go!"

"Have fun, kids," Kendra called. *Poor Eve.*

34

"They're gone," Brittany told Malory as soon as Heather and Eve left with their dates.

Malory stood in front of the open refrigerator drinking her private reserve of sour lemonade directly from the pitcher. "Good. Heather will make sure Caliban doesn't ruin our virgin." She put the pitcher back and shut the door. "Is everything ready for tonight?"

"Yes. Everything's ready. Michele and Teri are finishing up. So . . ."

"So, what?" Malory smiled.

"Can I go with you to visit Professor Tongue?"

"Yes. He even knows you're coming along this time."

"Really? You decided not to surprise him?"

"He's cooking. I had to tell him."

"We're getting sex *and* dinner?"

"We are. He's not a bad chef, either."

"What's he making?"

"Something Italian." Malory opened a cabinet above the counter and took something out. "We'll bring the nibbles."

"Honey-roasted peanuts!" Brittany exclaimed, stomach growling. "My favorite."

"I know. Come on, let's get out of here." She handed Brittany the nuts. "You can't open them until we get there."

"Okay. Malory? Why are you being so pleasant tonight?"

"I'm always pleasant when a sacrifice is coming up."

Brittany gave the can of nuts a quick shake. She loved the sound. "So, do you think Holly Gayle will come around?"

"That damned ghost. Of course she'll come around. She always does when we're sacrificing one of her own. The stupid, dead bitch!"

35

Around eight, Kendra finished her paper for McCobb. By nine she had read three of the four chapters assigned from other classes and written the beginning of a simple essay on government for a required and detested course. The professor could put sharks to sleep. She got up from the desk and did a few stretches, thought about going downstairs and socializing, but decided she'd rather have some downtime. Seeing the Gamma rule book on her bed, she fluffed up the bed's two pillows—*a definite improvement on the dorm room*—and arranged them to shield herself from the curving brass headboard, then plopped down and picked up the book. Looking at it—*assigned reading for a sorority!*—she wondered if joining Gamma wasn't a bad move.

She wasn't a joiner, but it was something she'd always planned to do, ever since she first heard the stories about Granny's granny. It sounded like such a grand thing when Granny told the stories; grand despite the mysteries and the ghost stories. Even now, she wasn't sure why joining this sorority was important. She suspected she was just proving some point about how, in the old days, her grannies worked for the girls in the sorority, but now times had changed and she was one of the chosen ones. *Whatever. No experience is ever a waste.* Granny's words. She wanted to tell her grandmother she had been accepted into the sorority, but knew Granny wouldn't be impressed. She'd ask her if she had lost her mind.

Maybe I have. But she'd met interesting people. Eve was a delightful revelation, an eye-opener, and she knew she was the same for Eve. She thought about the hysterics that were barely fended off and hoped that wasn't a sign of things to come. Eve had seemed a little neurotic all along, but that was normal. Everybody had quirks and rarely were they aware of them. She and Eve were going to have quite a ride, finding out each other's eccentricities and making compromises. They'd moved in so quickly, they hadn't discussed anything important about rooming together. Music could be a problem; she had no idea what Eve listened to and vice versa, but since neither brought more than a small radio/CD player with them, chances were it wouldn't matter much. *What if Eve had hauled in a bunch of boy band CDs? But she didn't. Don't look for trouble.*

Granny always said that too, but just moving into this house was looking for trouble. She thought of Holly Gayle. A haunt could be real trouble, especially if someone as sensitive as Eve was exposed. *I wonder where that room is that Granny saw Holly in?* She couldn't ask her directly; the old lady had a knack for seeing through things and she'd know something was up. *Maybe Mom knows.* She was unsure about asking her, though, as well since she wasn't happy about Gamma either and if Kendra brought up ghost stories, her oh-so-rational mother might let Granny's stories get to her. After all, she'd been raised on them.

"Oh, well," Kendra sighed. She opened the book and started reading.

Just after ten, there was a knock on the door. "Who's there?" Kendra called.

"It's me."

"Get in here, Eve!"

Her roommate came in. Closing the door behind her, she felt for a lock, then bent, looking for one.

"It's no use. There isn't a lock."

"Well, we should put one on right away. Anyone could just walk in on us."

"That's the idea." Kendra held up the rule book. "No locks. It's to teach us to have no secrets from our sisters and to respect one another's privacy, not because we have to, but because we *want* to. It's all in here." She rolled her eyes.

"Well, that's ridiculous. We have to have a lock."

"Grounds for expulsion, the book says."

Eve dropped her purse on her bureau, then picked up the wooden desk chair and carried it to the door. "I'm not sleeping in an unlocked room."

"Well, a chair isn't technically a lock. But wait—I think they're going to hit us with the real initiation tonight. That's why they wanted everyone in early."

"We already took the oath."

"But we haven't been put through hell yet."

"True." Eve hung her jacket up and started undressing. "Do you think they'll come after we're asleep?"

"I don't know. But I sure wouldn't wear pj's to bed tonight. I'm wearing my jeans and this Henley all night. My running shoes are staying on."

"Don't worry." Eve picked up the pair of jeans she'd worn while moving in and pulled them back on. She pulled a fresh short-sleeved pink T-shirt over her head, then grabbed her socks and Reeboks and put them on.

"You sure love pink."

"Sorry."

"Don't be sorry. I wasn't criticizing, just observing. How'd you feel in your sophisticated outfit tonight?"

"I'm so glad I wore it. I felt more confident than I usually do."

"You're a cheerleader. That's supposed to be the embodiment of self-confidence."

"It is—when I'm on the field. Otherwise, not that confident."

"You'll get there. How was the date?"

"What date? I really liked Heather until now. Tonight, she was like a bloodhound or something. She followed me to the bathroom."

"That's normal."

Eve tilted her head. "I know it's normal, but she didn't do it the normal way."

"What? She tried to wipe your ass for you?"

Eve snickered. "That's not what I mean. She just kept watching me. Staring at me."

"Maybe she likes you."

"Stop it. It was creepy. And when we were at the table, she just kept talking. Art and I hardly even got to talk, let alone get to know each other."

"So is he worth knowing?"

"I think so. It was hard to tell. Heather's date was a talker too. Between them, we just sat there and listened."

"What did they talk about?"

"School. Competitions. Football. The sorority." She sat back on her bed. "You know, I should have found that a lot more interesting than I did. I think you're influencing me."

"And is that a good thing or a bad thing?"

"Listen!"

"What?" Even as Kendra asked, she heard footsteps approaching. Someone pounded on the door to the next room. "Quick, put the chair back where it belongs! They're coming for us!"

36

First there were blindfolds. The four girls who pounded on their door and rushed in uninvited were hidden within green cowled robes. Eve saw them briefly, a flash of rich gold satin edging the sleeves and hood. Then two of them jumped her, and the other two descended on Kendra. While one tied her hands behind her back, the other blindfolded her.

"Kendra?" she called as they rushed her forward, her feet stumbling.

"Hang tight, Evie!" Kendra called after her. "You'll be okay!"

They pulled her down the hall and didn't even attempt to let her stay on her feet as they descended to the first floor. Her toes thumped over the risers, her captors grasping her arms tightly. They reached the first floor and silently let her gain her feet, then started moving again.

"Please slow down a little. You're hurting my arms! Please!"

No reply came, but the grips grew tighter and the pace sped up until she tripped more than she walked. She decided to try logic. "I have to cheer at the football game next week. I can't have bruises all over my arms! Please be—ow!"

She shut her mouth and tried to keep up. She didn't know the house very well, but was pretty sure they'd taken her past the main rooms and into the echoey kitchen. Abruptly, they halted. Eve heard a door open, felt cold dank air on her face.

On the move again, down a short narrow flight of stairs. The air seemed close and wet. It smelled of damp earth. They pulled her along and she did her best to keep up. Finally, they came to another set of stairs. These led upward. They pushed her ahead of them, never speaking.

A dozen steps up, the sisters once again moved up beside her and took her elbows. Here, she could smell a hint of long-gone wood smoke, a pleasant scent if it weren't for the very faint whiff of decayed flesh that laced it. Panic rose in her throat. She forced it back.

They marched her through the room, stopping again to open a door. This one creaked; old wood on rusty hinges. They took her through the doorway and she tripped on something covering the floor. From the smell, it was old straw. And something had died on it a long time ago.

Eve's captors undid the bindings on her hands. Just as she began rubbing them to get the blood flowing, they took them again and pulled them above her head. She heard chains. A key in a padlock. The lock snapping open.

"Please, no," she cried as they fitted the manacles over her wrists and locked them down. "You're not going to leave me in the dark, are you? Please! Please don't leave me." Chains moved, pulling her arms up until her elbows couldn't bend. Eve fought back terror. Silent tears soaked the blindfold. "Please don't leave me here in the dark. Please don't leave me alone."

Unbidden, images from her nightmare shot through her mind. Suddenly, she was certain that thing from her nightmare—*the green ghost*—had been real and that it would return as soon as they left her. It would choke her with its tongue. It would do worse, too. *Stop thinking like that. This is just an initiation. Just college girls. Don't be afraid. It'll be over soon!*

Someone undid the blindfold. "Thank you!" she gasped before the soft material left her face. "Thank you!"

The cloth was gone. She opened her eyes slowly, so the light wouldn't hurt them. But there was nothing except darkness so thick it nearly smothered her, only that and her captors.

A click. Suddenly, a face appeared, inches away, illuminated from below by a small flashlight. "Malory!"

Malory smiled her cold, cold smile.

A second click. "Don't forget me."

It was Brittany, grinning madly. "Are you comfortable?"

"No."

"I'm glad you told the truth," Malory said. "If you hadn't, I'd have to pull your arms up until you squeak."

37

"You are here to pledge as a sister of Gamma Eta Pi," a feminine voice intoned for at least the third time. And, for the third time since Kendra, still blindfolded, had been hustled into whatever place they'd chosen for the initiation rites, the voice droned on about honor and loyalty and the spirit of sisterhood. She could hear the other pledges shifting and breathing around her.

Standing in darkness, draped in a cowled robe and forbidden to speak, she wondered if either of the girls flanking her was Eve. She doubted it; she thought she would probably sense the presence of her new roommate.

"Everyone, kneel," the voice commanded.

Carefully, Kendra got to her knees. The voice didn't belong to Malory or Brittany, which was surprising; she thought Malory would delight in doing the ordering. Instead, Kendra was almost certain it was Heather who was commanding the new sisters. Maybe that was logical, since she was the rush chairman.

Someone coughed.

"Silence!" the voice thundered. "Silence, or suffer the consequences!"

"Excuse me," some brave soul said softly. "Could you tell us what the consequences are?"

"Tell you?" the voice asked. "No, we won't tell you. But we'll show you."

Mocking laughter came from all around. Kendra realized one of the sisters who laughed stood directly behind her.

"No pledges shall move. We will now remove your blindfolds."

Kendra heard the rustle of robes and then hands roughly untied the cloth covering her eyes.

All she had known about the room was that it had to be on the second floor. Now her eyes told her a little more. It was neither small nor large. Lit only by flickering candles, the octagonal walls appeared to be covered entirely in velvety dark green draperies. The pledges, faces shadowed by their cowls, knelt in a circle. Kendra tried to spot Eve, but it was impossible in the dim light. The full sisters, their identities also hidden by their robes, stood behind them, an outer circle. Three sisters stood farther back, one behind an elevated podium, the others on either side, arms crossed.

"Who spoke?" the one—*Heather*—behind the podium asked.

"I did."

"Rise."

The girl did.

"You were told not to speak. You disobeyed. What say you?"

"It was a reasonable question," the shadowed pledge replied.

"And so it was. Come forward and receive your answer."

The girl stepped up to the podium. The two sisters flanking the speaker moved quickly, pulling her robe from her.

It was little Lou, the new substitute cheerleader.

"Strip." Heather's words were ice.

"What?"

"More punishment will be received for each word you speak. Strip."

Reluctantly, Lou pulled off her pajama top. Candle light flickered over her small breasts.

"Strip."

"But—I'm not wearing underwear."

"Strip or suffer further punishment if the sisters must do it for you."

Lou's lower lip started trembling. Seeing a silent tear on run down her cheek as she bent to remove her pajama bottoms, Kendra looked away, embarrassed for her.

"Everyone keep your eyes on your sister!" Heather ordered. Whoever stood behind Kendra roughly yanked her head back up.

Finally, Lou stood naked before them all. After an excruciatingly long pause, Heather stepped down from behind the podium. "Bend over and hold your ankles," she ordered.

The girl whimpered, but did as she was told.

Nothing happened. No one moved. Finally, Heather held out one hand and one of her helpers turned and took something from the podium and handed it to her.

It was a paddle. *A god damned stupid paddle. The oldest initiation trick in the book.*

"You will receive your punishment silently," Heather said, raising the wooden paddle. "Every time you cry out, you will receive one more hit."

And so it began.

The swats were firm but not cruel; the only cruelty was the humiliation, and that was very cruel indeed. *What the hell am I doing here?* Kendra, aware of the sisters looming around them, reluctantly kept her mouth shut and her eyes on the scene before her. She felt like she was in the Nazi Youth fraternity scene from *Animal House.*

38

"How can I cheer if you hurt me?" Eve asked, fighting back tears. Her arms, stretched above her, hurt so much she could hardly stand it. But the darkness was even worse. *I won't let them see me cry! I won't!* "My muscles are sore from practice. They're cramping. I won't be able to cheer!"

"Genevieve," Malory said, her voice deepening to the depths of the voice in her nightmare. "You're all done cheering."

"You had your night of glory." Brittany chittered, a vile sound that hurt Eve's ears.

"I don't understand." *I won't cry! I won't!*

And then hands ran over her breasts, pinching and prodding. They moved lower, undid her jeans. Eve braced herself as the hands—they had to be Brittany's since Malory's face remained unmoving before her—slipped inside her jeans.

"How'd you like me to do you with a dildo so big you'll think you're going to be split open?" Brittany's fingers pushed lower, invading, probing.

"Please stop! I'm a virgin!"

Brittany cackled, but Malory's deep laugh was pure malevolence.

"Exactly the reason you're here, Genevieve. Brittany, stop it right now. If you break her maidenhead, I'll have your sweet little ass on a platter for my dinner."

The hand withdrew. Brittany sighed.

A darkness speckled with woozy dots of light swirled before Eve's eyes as she felt herself trying to slip away in a faint. She welcomed the relief, but Malory wafted something acrid under her nose, bringing Eve fully back to consciousness.

"No, no," Malory said, the voice deepening again. "I know that trick, my dear. You spoiled my fun last night. I barely got to explore you before your little mind ran away and tried to hide from me."

"That was you? How?" Eve bit her lip, trying not to cry, trying to think of a way out of this.

The light clicked out. "I thought you'd have known it was me by the sound of my voice." Pinprick green eyes began to glow in the darkness before her, growing quickly, the demonic slitted pupils taking form. She smelled the lake, the forest, all the dead things in the woods on its breath.

The eyes moved closer. The slimy cold tongue touched her lips, tried to work its way between her clenched teeth.

It's real. Eve's mind, trapped, whirled, filled with horror and repulsion. She couldn't think, couldn't breathe; all she could do was feel that fetid sticky tongue coating her with stinking mucous and saliva. She could almost feel her brain starting to crack, to break like an egg. It would happen soon. *Please, God, let it happen now! Let me go!*

It wouldn't be long before everything broke apart, and it would be sheer relief. She prayed for it.

39

The initiation seemed endless to Kendra.

After the paddling, each pledge was made to take communion while still on her knees. Kendra had been first and, in retrospect, was glad of it because she was one of the few who didn't know what was being put in her mouth.

She had nearly gagged when a small object was placed on her tongue and, before she swallowed, felt tiny legs moving on her taste buds. An insect, a small roach, probably, ran blinding down her throat, saving her the horror or crunching it. The sister who fed it to her gave her a sip of fruity wine as a chaser, and after that, the worst was over.

There were recitations in some corrupted form of Latin, each girl had to lift her robe and drop panties for a ceremonial *thank-you-ma'am-may-I-have-another*? paddling, but no one else's face was revealed. Kendra kept herself from losing her temper by telling herself stories about initiations in other cultures; this one, in comparison, was a walk in the park.

At last, blindfolds were reapplied. Kendra sensed lights coming on and smelled candles being extinguished. After being twirled a few times to make her lose her sense of direction, she—and the others, she could tell by the sounds—were given another drink. This one began to take effect even as the elder sisters led her back to her bedroom. By the time she was laid out on the bed, she was beyond speaking. She wanted to say good night to Eve, but she couldn't find the energy. Instead, she drifted off into dreamless sleep.

40

"She's here!" Brittany spat the words in her chipmunk voice.

Something seemed different to Eve, something lightened the syrupy thick atmosphere. The tongue withdrew and Eve opened her eyes, her thoughts abruptly coherent. *Rescue!* "Help!" she cried. "Help!"

"I told you she'd show up," Malory said. "That bitch."

"You were right," Brittany replied. "As usual."

A greenish white glow behind Malory shimmered and began to shift, wavering slowly until it began to take human form. Eve stared hard, not understanding until the form completed transformation into a wet-haired girl in a soggy old-fashioned white dress. The flashlights went out. Malory turned her horrible greenish visage toward the apparition.

"Holly Gayle," Eve whispered.

She looked utterly real, lit by an inner light so that she was like a photo cut out and placed on black paper. She smiled sadly at Eve and glided forward.

Eve. Sister, I will help—

Malory began to chant, Brittany replying in unintelligible counterpoint. The voice in Eve's head silenced and the ghost of Holly Gayle stopped advancing.

"No," Eve cried as the image began to retreat slightly. "Please help me, Holly! Please!"

The ghost disappeared an instant later.

"She gave up pretty easily," Brittany said.

"The old bitch."

"Please," Eve began.

"'Please, please, please.' Are you always this polite?" Malory spat, turning on her. "Or is that all you know how to say?"

"Why are you doing this?" Eve shut her eyes as Malory's phantom face loomed before her.

"You're the one, Genevieve. You will soon be with the real Forest Knight. He will do far more to you than my tongue will. He will take your virginity and then I will take your life and your soul and I will give it to him. And he will give me everything I need."

The tongue flicked over one closed eyelid, then the other, leaving sticky slime that acted almost like glue. Eve slowly forced her eyes open as the tongue moved down, exploring her neck, tasting behind her ear. "Get away from me," she ordered.

The demonic face came up. The tongue

touched her lips, then withdrew. "You dare to order me around, you little bitch?"

"Yes." Eve felt her mind cracking as she faced the eyes, unflinching now. "Yes, I dare. Who the hell do you think you are?"

"I'll show you."

And she did.

Eve's brain short-circuited, a broken toy. She floated up, fearless now, fearless and free. She saw her body sagging in its shackles, saw Malory and Brittany. Malory cursed, kicking Brittany, kicking Eve's lifeless body.

Eve! Leave that place while you can.

Holly Gayle's voice called to her to come outside. She hesitated just a few seconds longer, listening to the creatures below, then let herself drift toward the voice calling her name. She seeped through the walls of the old smokehouse and saw Holly Gayle standing in front of her.

Take my hand, Eve. We'll go to the lake and I'll tell you a story. Would you like that?

Yes.

Together, they drifted into the woods.

41

Kendra?

She awoke slowly, her head thick, her mind muddy. The room was in darkness, the window over her desk open so that the filmy curtains fluttered in the breeze, ghosts on the wind.

Kendra?

The initiation. *They drugged me.* It started to come back.

And then the voice again, calling her.

Kendra.

"Eve?" she said, sitting up slowly. "Evie?"

Feeling for the beside lamp switch but not finding it, she looked toward the door of their room. Eve stood there solemnly, still dressed in jeans and the pink T-shirt. "Evie, did you just come in?"

Kendra.

She heard Eve's voice but the girl's lips didn't move as she glided toward her.

Kendra. Help me!

Kendra felt icy air as Eve neared her; she felt the hairs on the back of her neck lift, full of static electricity. The room was dark. She could barely see the curtains fluttering. But Eve was as plain as day. Eve, whose mouth didn't move, who glided instead of walked.

Kendra!

Kendra screamed.

The Sorority
MERILYNN

Tamara Thorne

Membership is forever. . . .

At exclusive, isolated Greenbriar University, within the elite Gamma Eta Pi sorority, is a secret society known as the Fata Morgana. Its members are the most powerful women on campus—and the deadliest. For this is a sisterhood of evil, a centuries-old coven, and every girl who pledges herself to their wicked decadence does so for life . . . or death. . . .

NOT EVERY DREAM IS SWEET

An old soul—that's what everyone calls dreamy, mystical Merilynn. Since childhood, she's had a sixth sense she can't explain, an ability to see things before they happen. Her psychic gifts tell her there's a tremendous darkness at work inside the shadowy walls of her sorority house—a feeling that intensifies when Malory Thomas invites her to become one with the Fata Morgana. Now, as she's drawn into the ever-tightening, unnatural circle of its sisterhood, Merilynn's dreams grow more alarming night by night, showing maddening glimpses of an evil, timeless bond stretching back through centuries of blood, sacrifice, and sexual magic. And soon Merilynn wonders whether this is a vision of the past—or a warning of very bad things to come. . . .

Applehead Lake
Cheerleading Camp

EIGHT YEARS AGO

1

"A long time ago, the town of Applehead was located right there under the lake." Counselor Allie Mayhew pointed toward the lake, its black water slowly rippling with silver moonlight.

Merilynn Morris, sitting on a log across the crackling campfire from Annie, shivered with delight and anticipation, then glanced at the other campers gathered on the circle of logs. Most of the pre-teen girls were saucer-eyed with pleasurable terror, though a few, like Eve Camlan, looked honestly afraid. And then there was Sam Penrose, beside Merilynn. Sam looked—well, she looked bored.

But Merilynn knew that was just a façade, Sam's usual nothing-bothers-me attitude. After yesterday's trip to the island, how could it be anything else? She hadn't been able to talk to Sam or Eve today, to find out what they were really thinking about the previous day's adventures, but she didn't have to be a genius to know that both of them were avoiding her. They didn't want to talk about it. *Chickens!*

"Everyone knew the town was going to be flooded," Allie Mayhew went on. "And even though most people were a little sorry about losing their orchards and their old homes, they understood that their valley was the only logical place for a reservoir and that because of the drought that had plagued them for four years already, their trees would die of thirst anyway.

"So they moved, leaving their homes and apple trees behind. Many left and helped found the little village of Crackle Hill—"

"That's Caledonia now," some camper blurted.

"That's right, Megan," Allie said, nodding. "Others went farther north or south, but the people who really loved the valley and this forest, they stayed right here."

"*Right* here?" Merilynn prompted. *Get to the ghost stories already!*

"Yes, some did. The main house where we have our meals and indoor meetings here at camp once belonged to a family named Gayle. Mr. and Mrs. Gayle had just one daughter and after she died, they moved away, willing the property to Greenbriar University."

"How did Holly Gayle die?" Merilynn prompted.

"You're a glutton for ghost stories, Merilynn," Allie said, smiling. "We've already told the story of Holly. She drowned."

"You've only told it twice." Merilynn looked around for support from her fellow campers. "Have *you* ever seen her ghost?"

Girls murmured, titillated.

"Me?" Allie asked.

Merilynn nodded.

Everyone stared at the counselor, who looked around, as if checking to make sure no one else was listening. Many of the girls turned their heads, too, nervously, probably more worried about Holly's ghost than eavesdropping counselors. In absolute heaven, Merilynn asked, "Have you, Allie? Have you seen her?"

"Well . . . Maybe."

Hushed gasps hissed through the air. The firelight wavered.

"No," Allie added. "I can't really say I saw her. I just imagined it, I'm sure."

"Oh, come on, Allie," Merilynn urged. "Tell us anyway."

"Well . . ." She looked at the girls appraisingly. "It was last summer."

Tell! Tell! Tell! Merilynn could barely sit still.

"It was early September, the day after the last campers left for home. Only we—the counselors—were still here, cleaning up and closing things up for the season. That last night, we had the guys—the counselors from the football camp across the lake," she pointed, "over for our annual party. They drove over. It was still light out, only about six o'clock, when they arrived, but you know how these woods are. It seemed dark."

Allie paused dramatically, then glanced at her

wristwatch. "It's late. Maybe I should finish the story tomorrow night—"

Girls moaned and begged, which Merilynn knew was just what she wanted. Allie was her favorite counselor because she loved telling stories.

"Okay. There were nearly two dozen of us altogether, us and the guys. We had a barbeque and then we all sat right here and toasted marshmallows over the campfire."

"Did you drink?" Sam Penrose asked, doing her Spocky-eyebrow thing.

"Drink?" Allie asked. Then, shocked, "You mean alcohol?"

"Yes."

"Of course not! That's not allowed!"

Bullpuckies, thought Merilynn, trying not to grin too much. She knew right where they hid the beer and wine coolers. So did Sam. They'd found the treasure trove together, hidden in an old hollow log. She launched an elbow into Sam's arm to keep her from saying so. It might be fun to see Allie's reaction, but it would ruin the ghost story.

Sam returned the poke so hard that Merilynn had to stifle a yelp. They exchanged a look. Merilynn knew the girl wouldn't tell.

"So, what happened?" Sam asked. "Did someone pretend to be a ghost while you were toasting your marshmallows?"

Merilynn poked her again, glared at her. "Don't spoil this," she whispered.

Sam crossed her eyes at her, but nodded in acquiescence.

"It wasn't while we were around the campfire," Allie said at last. "It was later. Down by the dock."

Everyone turned their heads toward the little dock poking out into the lake, rowboats leashed to it like puppy dogs. There was a small boathouse too, on the far side of the dock, but it was rarely used during camping season. At the moment, it was nothing but a dark smudge on the narrow beach.

"It was probably ten or eleven and we'd split up, you know, to walk around."

A couple of the more knowledgeable girls giggled. Allie silenced them with her own silence.

"Nothing bad was going on," she said. Merilynn knew she had to say that, then Sam leaned over and whispered, "Condoms," in her ear.

Merilynn just about lost it. To keep from laughing, she pinched the back of her hand until tears sprung into her eyes. She was going to have to get Sam later. Sam was definitely messing with her.

"One of the guys and I were walking along the beach and we decided to go sit on the pier. We walked to the end then sat down and took off our shoes so we could dangle our feet in the water.

"It was really dark. Darker than it is now. We were just talking and kind of looking down into the water. Way, way out, I saw a light come on under the water. One, then another."

Oohs and ahs, hushed, almost reverent, punctuated her pause.

"The other counselor saw them too. We looked at each other and he said, 'You know what that means?' and I said, 'What?'"

"What?" several girls murmured.

"He said the town was coming to life." Allie looked from girl to girl before adding, "'When the town starts coming to life,' he told me, 'that means Holly Gayle is taking a walk.'"

Merilynn saw Eve Camlan draw into herself, hugging herself with her arms. She felt sorry for her, being so afraid. But not that sorry. "And then you saw the ghost?" she asked Allie.

"Not yet. I got nervous. I mean, who wouldn't?"

Campers nodded enthusiastically.

"So I told Mark—the guy I was with—that we were just seeing starlight reflected on the water. He said maybe so.

"I stood up and said I was cold, you know, to get him to get off the pier." Flames glittered in Allie's wide eyes. "I mean, it was late, and those lights looked real, even if they weren't. I just couldn't stand having my feet in the water then, because I just *knew* one of Holly Gayle's cold, dead white arms was going to reach out of the water and grab my ankle and pull me in!"

A lot of girls looked frightened now, and Merilynn leaned forward, enthralled. "What happened? What did you see?"

"Well, I pulled my sandals on and Mark got up.

He teased me a little, but was pretty quick putting his own shoes back on." Allie smiled for an instant, cut it off abruptly. "We turned around to walk back down the pier. And then it happened. We saw her."

Shocked inhalations, breaths held.

"And?" Merilynn said.

"She came out of the boathouse at the shoreline, right where we'd have to pass to get off the dock. For a minute, I thought she was just one of the other counselors. But she was wearing a long white dress. *Holly*, I thought. Mark stopped walking and just stared. Me too. And then I was positive again it was just one of the counselors pretending to be Holly. I mean, isn't that what you'd think?"

She looked right at Merilynn.

"No," Merilynn said, throwing Allie off, loving it. "I'd think it was the ghost."

"Well, Merilynn," Allie said, fear actually showing in her eyes now, "You might have been right. The girl in the white dress seemed to be walking—but too smoothly, like maybe she wasn't quite touching the ground. She was coming toward the lake. I mean, really, she looked like she was *on* it, but that's impossible."

"If it was a ghost, it's not impossible," Merilynn said.

Girls giggled, clutching one another now.

"Well, Mark and I thought it was a joke, so we just made ourselves head right toward her. You know, to get off the pier. As we got to the boat-house and the shore, though, the girl just vanished. Faded away into thin air. But before she was gone, I saw her face and hair. She was wet, her hair just hung around their face like she'd been in the lake. Her dress, too. I could see water dripping off her fingertips. And her face . . ."

Silence.

"It wasn't one of the counselors. I'd never seen her before."

Campers jabbered in soft tones, telling each other what they wanted to hear. Merilynn briefly caught Eve Camlan's gaze, saw the horror in her eyes, and sent her the gentlest smile she had. Then she rose and left the circle, walking twenty feet to the lake's edge.

The dark water rippled with silver moonlight. It was hard to be sure, but Merilynn thought she caught brief glimmers of deep golden light far out beneath the surface.

"Holly?" she whispered. "Holly, where are you?"